REPRESENT

WRITTEN BY
DAVID L.

Represent By David L.

Copyright © 2010 David L.
Printed in the United States

All Total Package Publications, LLC titles are available at special quantity discounts for bulk purchases for sales promotions, premiums, fundraisers, educational and/or institutional use. Visit www.totalpackagepublications.com for ordering information.

Any resemblances of people, places, or events are unintentional and truly coincidental.

Published by Total Package Publications, LLC
Edit and layout by Carla M. Dean
Printed by United Graphics, Inc., Mattoon, IL
Cover Design by Deneen Robinson

ISBN: 978-0-9789276-3-9
LCCN: 2010903294

Sales inquiries should be forwarded to:
Total Package Publications, LLC
P.O. Box 3237
Mount Vernon, NY 10553

ALSO AVAILABLE BY DAVID L.:

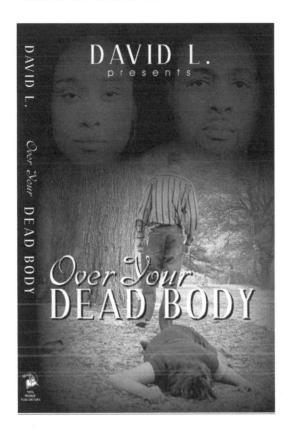

Over Your Dead Body
ISBN#: 978-0-9789276-0-8

"The plot is well formulated and the tension never ceases. Once you start reading this book, you can't stop!"
~Alice Holman, Raw Sistaz Book Reviewers

ALSO AVAILABLE BY DAVID L.:

Chalk Outline Confessions
ISBN#: 978-0-9789276-1-5

"An entertaining psychological thriller that will leave you anticipating another novel from David L."
~Radiah Hubbert, Urban-Reviews.com

ALSO AVAILABLE BY DAVID L.:

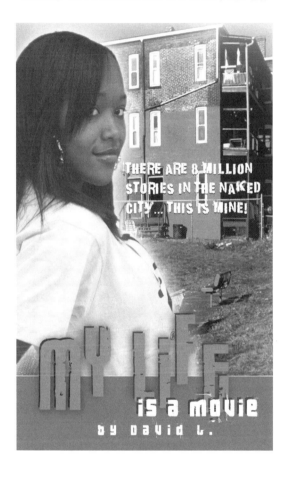

My Life is a Movie
ISBN#: 978-0-9789276-2-2

"Pleasantly surprised! I was thrust right into the storyline!"
~Sistar Tea, ARC Book Club

REPRESENT

WRITTEN BY
DAVID L.

PRELUDE

T he courtroom is the last place I wanted to spend my Friday morning, but unfortunately, fate has dealt my family this hand. So, I don't have much choice in the matter. In a few minutes, it will be my turn to testify on my brother's behalf. The mostly white jurors are looking over at him with a hint of disdain as they listen to the testimony from my brother's high-priced lawyer. As powerful a speaker as he is, the prosecuting attorney seems to be just a little bit more inspired. Probably because the entire state of New York has been trying for so long to make some of my brother's charges stick. The irony about the whole thing is maybe my brother really is innocent this time. Maybe - but somehow, I seriously doubt it!

My entire family is wrapped up in the drug game, and has been since before I was conceived. Everyone has a hand in it except me – and I plan on keeping it that way. I'm not built for a life of crime, and I doubt very seriously I can make it in a cell with nothing around but convicts looking for their next package…or next human conquest.

I'm halfway to getting my Bachelor's Degree in Psychology

David L.

at Fordham University, and I am the starting wide receiver on a semi-pro football team that plays its home games in a posh neighborhood in Clinton Hills, Brooklyn. I may even land an NFL contract in a year or two if I can showcase my talents at next week's game. Word on the streets is over a dozen NFL scouts are going to be there to check for me and a rival of mine, Kerry Mourning. He's the starting tailback for the Bronx Banshees and averages over seven yards a carry. He also leads the semi-pro division in punt returns.

My brother Trenton, better known to everyone in the neighborhood and beyond as "Innocent" because he's been cleared of over twenty-seven charges in a three year span, is looking confident as usual. His lawyer is now whispering something in his ear, and he responds by whispering something back. It's the first, maybe second time, I've ever seen my brother in a suit. It's almost as if he knows his luck is finally running out. No. I can't even begin to think like that. My brother has beaten every other charge, and this one should be no different.

Everyone in the courtroom turns around in unison as my father, Forrester Mitchell a.k.a. "Crime", enters the courtroom and takes a seat away from the rest of the family. He's a man whose presence demands respect, and even the gravelly voice of Judge Camarillo cannot take away from the obvious distraction my father has just caused. Knowing him, he probably hired a limousine service to bring him here from his mansion in Connecticut. Ever since I could remember, he has done everything in style and flair. Once when I was twelve, he pulled up to my peewee football game and parked his spanking new Mercedes Benz on the grass where everyone was getting ready to play! The referees and opposing players literally begged him to find somewhere else to park. That's how he is. That's how he will always be. A showstopper - plain and simple - until the day he dies.

The courtroom is now almost filled to capacity as Judge

Camarillo desperately tries to reclaim the cooperation from the people sitting in the back row. Even some of the local media is present to see my brother's streak of getting exonerated of all criminal charges possibly come to a screeching halt.

My sister Tammy is sitting across from me and is trying to tell me something, but I can't quite read her lips. Seated next to her is her low-life boyfriend who has never worked an honest job in his life. Even when my pops and Innocent offered him a job working at their trucking company, he turned it down. Although my father and brother's business is a front so they can transport illegal drugs interstate, as well as look legit in the eyes of the law, it can be a lucrative way to generate an income. He is a leech by nature, yet smart enough to know that when you're connected to my family, you instantly raise your stock in the hood.

An elderly woman seated directly behind Trenton yells out some obscenities and is threatened by a court officer that she will be removed if her actions do not immediately cease. It's a scene directly out of New Jack City, except the only difference is this woman doesn't pull out a gun and shoot my brother. Not yet anyway.

Trenton remains calm and sits with his hands folded. He has a smug smile on his face, but I know my brother better than anyone in the courtroom. He has to be slightly nervous. He is potentially moments away from having his freedom taken away for an undetermined amount of time.

One by one, testimonies are delivered by witnesses from all over, and each is given a hard look by my brother as they exit the witness stand. One forty-something-year-old male gives his testimony and directly implicates my brother to several of the shootings that have been taking place throughout Brooklyn. From the corner of my eye, I see Trenton holding up his hand, making the sign of a gun with his thumb and index finger as the man exits the witness stand. Although I'm only vaguely familiar with the drug game, I've got enough sense to know this guy has just been marked for death. Where I'm from, a snitch is the lowest form of life, and this guy is most definitely a snitch who will be dealt with eventually by Trenton or one of his many goons.

The moment of truth closes in, and although they have no legal right to force me to talk since he is my immediate family, I agree nonetheless to enter the witness stand. I wish my mother was still alive to see this day. It may sound crazy, but she was real big on all of us standing strong together to combat a common enemy. Even if that "enemy" was the U.S. legal system. She had a good life and was a martyr in the community. She did everything from sponsoring troubled youth so they could attend community outings to purchasing real estate so low-income mothers with newborn infants had a place to live and not have to reside in a shelter.

Halfway to the witness stand, I look over at my brother and my legs become numb with anxiousness. Although he's beaten his share of cases in the past, I can't help but think that no one is untouchable – not even my brother.

My time on the witness stand was not as monumental as I had imagined. The prosecuting attorney tried to thwart my intelligence with a string of illogical questions; however, I persevered. Once he realized I was far from a novice relating to the extracurricular affairs of my brother, I was asked to step down from the witness stand.

Trenton's lawyer requested an adjournment, but that request fell on deaf ears from the judge who has a visible dislike for my brother. That's when it finally hit me. No way was Trenton getting out of this one. All of the signs were there: a jury full of white people, an unsuccessful delay of the trial, and a judge who was notorious for his harsh sentencing on minority males. Even with my brother's astounding luck with getting off and the best lawyer money can buy, he still had two strikes against him. That meant one more strike and he was finished for good.

Many of Trenton's supporters are getting antsy, and just

when things couldn't get any more chaotic, Crystal waltzes into the courtroom. She is my brother's long-term girlfriend slash baby mama. I can't really say anything bad about her because she has always been there for him. It's just that she can be very dramatic at times. It's a Kodak moment as she finds a seat next to my father because they are both so similar. She has the influence and aura that almost matches the size of my father, and also like him, she doesn't take no mess when it comes to holding down her family. It's too bad my little nephew isn't with her. He is only three years old and already patterning himself after his father. This time next year, he'll probably be running his daycare center!

The mighty blow of the judge's gavel emanates throughout the courtroom as Judge Camarillo hands down his verdict: GUILTY.

As half the courtroom sighs in relief, the other half grits their teeth in anger. Trenton has a look on his face as if he is about to take a swing at his lawyer. My sister is in tears, as is Crystal, so much to the point that Crystal has to be restrained by two very large court officers. Unable to regain her composure, she is promptly removed from the courtroom. Surprisingly, my father remains in his seat motionless and void of emotion.

After all of the terrible things Trenton has done – all of his acts of violence – it is all coming to an end. How many years you ask? Life without the possibility of parole. The charges? Three counts of racketeering; three counts of manslaughter; two counts of first-degree murder; two counts of bribery; one count of evading arrest; one count of perjury; one count of reckless endangerment, and one count of driving with a suspended license. Talk about a rap sheet! They didn't even bother trying to nail him on any direct drug-related charges. And that's just the stuff they knew about! I shake my head in disbelief as the guilty verdict is played over and over again in my mind.

Trenton doesn't put up any struggle as he is unceremoniously cuffed by a nearby court officer. While being escorted out of the courtroom, he looks over at me and nods his head. That's his "everything is going to be alright" head nod. Just like my brother. Here he is facing a life sentence, and he's shaking it off like it's nothing more than a weekend stay at juvenile detention.

Even with my father seated in the back row and my sister sobbing uncontrollably on my shoulders, I've never felt so alone in my life. Trenton was the proverbial glue that held the family down since my father bounced to Connecticut several years ago. And now all is lost. I should've seen this coming.

CHAPTER ONE

"**Y**o, Trip, make that phone call to your connect right now. If dude don't have my money, him and I are gonna have some serious problems. That's on my life!"

"I got you. Don't even sweat it. I left son a message like three hours ago. I know him. He's not stupid to try and play me like that. He knows better than to mess around with your money."

"Oh, so now you're holding him down? You gonna cover for him if I don't get my cash?"

"I mean…"

"That's what I thought! Get me my money! Or else I'm holding you personally responsible!"

My brother Innocent and his right-hand man Trip were having a "friendly debate" over some money owed from a local business associate. If it's one thing my brother has never tolerated, it's not having all of his money on time. I'm not a betting man, but I would give all the money in my pocket that Innocent had all of his money before the day was over. I can remember an occasion a couple of years ago when someone

David L.

came up short with his money. My brother made a spectacle out of the individual by making him walk home butt-ass naked. And the man was only short by ten dollars!

"How much money came in today?" Innocent questioned.

"At least three thousand…give or take."

"Give or take? Man, you better count that money again and give me an exact amount!"

"My fault. I'll count it right now."

"You're starting to worry me, Trip. You're slacking. I can't be having that from my first-in-command. Do I need to replace you with one of these cats out here on the block hungry for a job promotion?"

Doing as he was instructed, Trip counted all the money that was made so far that day on a very cold and windy afternoon. Trip and Innocent were inside Trip's apartment, but they still found themselves rubbing their hands together for warmth. It was beginning to get colder, and for someone who considered himself a baller, the least Trip could do was pay his Con Ed bill!

"Three thousand one hundred and seventy dollars, just like I said."

"Don't play with me, Trip! I want everything accounted for down to the very last cent. I got people to pay off and mouths to feed. If it's one thing I've learned in this business, it's to never cheat anybody. That's why my rep is so on point."

"I hear you loud and clear. It won't happen again."

"It better not."

While Innocent instructed Trip to count the money for the second straight time, he pulled out a razor blade from a drawer in the kitchen and began cutting up his product into cube-size shapes. Then he placed them into a tiny envelope, ready for sale. From there, each envelope was personally stamped by Innocent so the fiends in the neighborhood knew the product they were getting from my brother's team was official.

Thirty minutes went by, and because his last count was off by ten dollars, Innocent made Trip count their stash once again.

Then again for one hundred percent accuracy. A word of caution…my brother never took kindly to his money being funny. He had already made it painfully clear to Trip on more than one occasion that neither one of them were going anywhere until all of the money added up correctly.

Both Trip and my brother spent the next forty-five minutes counting up the money to make sure everything added up in the freezing cold apartment, but knowing my brother, things would begin to heat up soon enough.

I was a little more than halfway through the fall semester and had three papers to complete in less than a week. I had gotten to that point in my studies by procrastinating until the last minute, so why change what worked? As long as I was able to maintain at least a "B" average, I qualified for advanced standing and would be able to begin my Master's program as long as I obtained a passing grade in my remaining papers that were due.

Yep, you guessed it. I was the nerd of the family. The one who never took a risk and played it safe his entire life. While Innocent and the rest of my family were slinging drugs throughout the five boroughs of New York and beyond, I had my head buried in the books. Even my father had mixed emotions when I told him about my plans to attend college and study psychology. But then what could you expect from a man who went by the moniker of "Crime"?

My father, Forrester "Crime" Mitchell, was a bonafide living legend in the neighborhood where I grew up. Always a force to be reckoned with, the other hustlers idolized him. Although he moved out to Greenwich, Connecticut several years ago when things started getting hot for him, he always

David L.

kept his ears to the street. That's how things were done in my family. He ran the hood with an iron fist, and even after a self-imposed "semi-retirement" from the drug business, he proudly handed the title over to my brother Innocent.

"We need to find us some chicks to type our paper for us. That's the only way we're going to get through this semester."

That was my boy Tyrone talking. He and I met freshman year and had been in almost every class together.

"Nah, that ain't my style. Anything I do, I do myself."

"Whatever. You won't be talking that mess after you've been up all night working on that twenty-page report for clinical psychology."

"You're right. This is one paper I'm not gonna wait to do until the last minute. I'm heading to the library right now to get started on it."

That was my life at the time. Writing papers for school and once a week, playing football for the Brooklyn Cyclones. While I was busy trying to graduate, and maybe get a tryout with an NFL team down the line, my brother and the rest of my family were grossing close to twenty thousand dollars a week. I really began to wonder if I was in the right business.

November 16th - It was my born day, and instead of cradling a beer somewhere in a club with my closest friends, I was contemplating my classmate Tyrone's suggestion on getting a female in my class to write my paper. A few hours earlier, I was dead set against it, but as I ran the track with three more laps to go, it was beginning to make a lot more sense.

I had just finished stomach crunches, catching drills with the wide receivers' coach, and running the stairs under the bleachers. I'm a loner by nature and most of my teammates never paid me too much attention, except for a couple of the fellas on offense...my homeboys Felix and Big Mike. Felix was a speedy Hispanic cat who, if given an open lane in the backfield, would go the distance before the blink of an eye. Big Mike was a behemoth. Six-foot-four and three hundred pounds

18

of raw strength. He was committed to getting an NFL tryout by any means necessary and probably will eventually on just his tenacity alone. There was a rumor from within the team that he had experimented with steroids, but he had sworn there was absolutely no truth to the rumor. He had never been tested because there was no testing for illegal substances at that level of football. To his credit, he had never displayed any of the well-known signs of steroid abuse: mood swings, loss of hair, or outbursts of "roid rage".

"What do you think of that quarterback we're going up against Saturday?" Felix questioned.

"I think we're in trouble if our defense don't step up and do their thing," Big Mike responded.

"You just protect your side of the line and buy me some time to get open. I'll make 'em pay!" I assured both of my teammates.

Coach Stevens was a defensive-minded man, so our defensive teammates were often the last ones to leave the field. Each of the offensive players, including myself, privately waved at them as we exited the field and headed to our cars in order to get home and take a refreshing hot shower. I told myself the current semester would be over in a little over a month, and I would be able to focus on football a little bit more. Hell, by that time the following year, I may even have had the chance to work in my field and work toward obtaining my Master's Degree...maybe even my Doctorate. Those types of aspirations were a rarity for a kid who bolted out of high school for two and a half years to work as a delivery man for a mid-sized messenger company.

Before that day ended, I had promised to treat myself to something special. Even though none of my family called to wish me happy birthday, I was in too much of a high-spirited mood to hold it against them. It's not every day a man in my neighborhood got to celebrate his twenty-first birthday without having at least one foot in the grave.

Elsewhere, Innocent had been eyeing the new 2010 Range Rover for several weeks and had just pulled up to the car dealership with Trip by his side to check one out. He had been talking about it for several months and swearing to anyone who would listen that he would be the first brother in the hood behind the wheel of one.

Notice I specifically used the word "eyeing". My brother was no window shopper by any means. If he saw something he wanted, he would buy it straight cash with no questions asked. He liked to do things big, and the metallic silver Range he was about to test drive was no exception. His presence was immediately felt as he walked through the front door, and in less time than it took to blink an eye, an overzealous salesman approached him with his arm outstretched to shake his hand.

"What can I interest you in today?" the salesman questioned.

"That silver Range in the lot. The one with the windows already tinted and the chrome rims."

"That's a good choice. That one comes fully loaded, and it's a steal when you consider all of the features it comes with."

"What about navigation system?" Trip added in.

"That's an optional feature. But, for literally a few extra dollars a month, you wouldn't even notice it in your monthly payment."

Innocent and Trip looked at each other and laughed at the salesman's monthly payment comment.

"Nah! No monthly payments for me," Innocent responded. "I'm strictly a 'cash upfront' type of dude. I don't do the blue-collar, working-man finance thing. And before you even mention leasing, forget it. I don't do leases either."

"Well then, let me go and get the keys so we can take it out for a test drive. I just need to make a copy of your driver's license."

My brother's license had been suspended for well over a year. So, as soon as the salesman announced he couldn't take the Range out for a test drive without it, he quickly walked over to the corner with Trip to huddle and discuss their next course of action. A few minutes passed, and after convincing Trip to test drive the Range in his place, they both departed the lot with the salesman. As expected, it was a smooth drive, and after giving it a thorough look over, Innocent promised to return the following day to complete the sale. He even went as far as to hand the salesman five crisp one-hundred-dollar Franklins to ensure no one came in after him to purchase his soon-to-be ride.

"Don't forget the plan," Innocent said to Trip.

"I'm not going to forget. I'll be back down here tomorrow morning with the money, and I'll put the Range in my name. Don't worry. I got you! But, you really do need to get your license situation taken care of. What if you get pulled over?"

"Don't worry about me, son. As long as I got cops in Brooklyn in my pocket, I'm always gonna be good."

I had spoken too soon when I made the assumption that no one remembered my birthday. An eerie feeling engulfed me as I grabbed the knob of my apartment door. I hesitated momentarily before turning it. Sure enough, a few familiar faces – and some not so familiar – were looking at my shocked expression as my sister Tammy embraced me with a hug. I was quickly hugged again by my girlfriend, Angel. She and my sister didn't always see eye to eye and had privately fought over my affection. Typical female drama. I think it dated back to me not being in the family business. Angel always said my family

was a bad influence and that I should distance myself from
them. Tammy, on the other hand, thought Angel was stuck up
and full of herself. Truth be told – they were both right!

"Don't just stand there looking crazy! So were you surprised
or what?" Tammy asked.

"Hell yeah, I was surprised! Y'all got me good! I thought
for sure you forgot it was my birthday."

"You know I could never forget my baby's birthday," Angel
blurted out.

I could see my sister roll her eyes in response to Angel's
comment, but no way was I going to let their petty bickering
interfere with my day.

"So where are all my presents?"

"This surprise birthday party is your present, fool!" Tammy
responded.

She wasn't kidding either. With the exception of some
bottles of Hennessey and Bacardi Rum that laced my dining
room table, I didn't see a gift anywhere in sight. Not like I
needed anything to cement my worth. Innocent and my father
had been very generous throughout the years, and with the
exception of paying for my school tuition, I wanted for nothing.

I was soon greeted with more random hugs from my guests.
Sometimes I swear my sister didn't think when she planned a
party. Nicole, one of my ex-girlfriends who got an invite,
walked over to plant a wet one on the side of my cheek. Or
maybe it was my sister's plan to get my girl jealous. We shared
some small talk for a very brief amount of time, and it wasn't
until she began dropping subtle hints about hooking up with me
that I told her I had to go and greet the rest of my guests. Nicole
was one of those ex-girlfriends that I knew I could get with if I
so desired. Unfortunately for her, I no longer had any interest in
old a** from back in the day.

Although visibly late, two of my best friends from junior
high school arrived to show me some love – Kevin a.k.a.
"Swift" and Tone Greene. The past couple of years, we hadn't

seen that much of one another. One, I had been too busy with school; two, we had been hanging in different circles; and three, they were low-level drug runners for one of my brother's rivals on the other side of Brooklyn.

"The two of you are looking real suspect right about now," I said.

"Whatcha mean?" Tone replied.

"I mean, how you gonna show your faces at my place with no present?"

"At least we showed up!" Swift chimed in.

I was privately grateful that they showed up when they did, because my ex Nicole was starting to get real blatant with her advances towards me.

The guests finally left and the party was over. El finito. I looked around in amazement and contemplated cleaning up, but I was way too inebriated from the six shots of Hennessey that I was forced to consume – courtesy of Tone and Swift. My ghetto-a** sister made me take a shot with her, as well. She later apologized for Trenton's absence and blamed it on him forgetting. Just like my sis to keep it real and tell it like it really is.

"You got a look on your face like you want to throw up."

That was Angel. The only one left from the party. The only one I wanted left from the party. Could you blame me? It was great having my people over to celebrate my born day, but the party was over and it was time to get some drawers from my lady.

"Me? Throw up? Girl, you're talking to the original Henny guzzler!"

"Don't front for me like I've never seen you hugging the toilet before. Just a couple of months ago, you were throwing up after a wild night out with the fellas. Swearing to me that you were never gonna drink again. Remember that night?"

"You wrong for that. Why you gotta bring that up again?"

"Just keeping it real. Now go lay down in the bed and wait a few minutes for me to freshen up. I'm going to slip into something, and I'll be in to give you your real birthday present."

That's all I needed to hear. Angel's "friend" had been lingering for the past few days, so up until her birthday present comment, I wasn't quite sure if I was going to get any. I went into my customary ritual of push-ups and sit-ups before getting under the covers. My anticipation was at an all-time high as I patiently waited for her to exit the bathroom.

"I'll be out in a minute," Angel yelled out. "You're still up, right?"

Oh, I was up alright. In more ways than she could imagine. I had been waiting for almost a week to get me some. Lying in bed was causing the room to start spinning, and I could taste the Hennessey whenever I burped.

"Hurry up!" I yelled in response.

The spinning sensation increased and even closing my eyes didn't do me any good. Angel emerged from the bathroom similar to her namesake. She was wearing nothing but a pair of white panties and a matching white teddy. Definitely worth the wait.

"You like what you see?" she asked, as if she didn't already know my answer.

Angel was eyeing me seductively and waiting at the corner of the bed to see what my next move would be. *Do I just lay here and wait for her advances or do I pounce on her like a lion on its prey?* I did neither.

Just as Angel slid under the covers, I quickly threw the covers off of me and made a dash into the bathroom. My romantic night came to a screeching halt as I let out the contents of my night into the porcelain bowl. Equally frustrated, Angel could do nothing but turn over in disgust and go to sleep. I, on the other hand, once again swore to myself that my drinking days were a thing of the past.

CHAPTER TWO

O ut in the projects near the Polo Grounds area in Harlem, Innocent and Trip made a necessary pit stop to take care of some last-minute business with a close family associate of my pops.

"He's never been late before. It's not like him," Innocent announced.

Just as the words were uttered, headlights could be seen from a distance, signaling Trevor's arrival. Trevor was an old family connect that had been doing business with my family for well over a decade. He was an older cat – at least in his mid forties – who used to do side jobs with my father. He had a raspy voice and was never seen without the latest trendy outfit or a bad a** woman by his side.

"That him?" Trip questioned.

"Yeah, that's him. I can spot his flashy-a** car from miles away!"

"And you trust him?"

"What? Yeah, I trust him! He's had my father's back before I even got into the business. Back when the truck company was a legit company. My pops swears by him…and so do I."

Trevor was a slender, tall cat. Like Innocent, he had an imposing presence, and although Trip and my brother were basically inseparable, Trip was obviously the odd man out in their dealings with one another.

"You sure nobody followed you here?" Trip questioned.

Trevor didn't bother to respond to Trip's inquiry. Instead, he continued his conversation with Innocent. Over seven thousand in cash was handed to Trevor, and in return, my brother was handed a shopping bag full of cocaine and other drug paraphernalia. Another bag, which appeared to be at least five pounds of marijuana, was presented to Innocent from out of the trunk of Trevor's car. Trip was fuming because Innocent didn't even bother to check out the contents of what was just given to him. Instead, Trevor and Innocent sealed their deal with a handshake and an old story about how Crime once duped the cops during a high-speed chase out in Long Island a while back.

"I wanted you to meet one of my boys, but I guess he's a no-show," Trevor reasoned.

"I thought I met all your main contacts. Who is it?" Innocent questioned.

"I wanted it to be a surprise. You know how I like to pull a fast one on you every now and then. Oh well, maybe next time."

"You know how much I hate surprises. Who is it?"

"This must be your surprise," Trip interrupted.

"Surprise my a**! That looks like one of them new undercover vehicles the cops are riding around in. That mutha***** is five-0!" Innocent said in anger.

"Oh s**t! This mutha***** set us up!" Trip said.

Neither my brother nor Trip knew what to do. Their minds told them to make a run for it, but their legs were frozen in shock. Sure enough, the undercover cop car inched closer, and what looked to be a plain-clothes officer stepped out and stood in place for about a minute. A white undercover who stood out in Harlem like a sore thumb. Innocent always knew that as long as he led this kind of life, it could possibly lead to this. He just never imagined it would go down quite like this. Not so soon anyway.

"I swear I'm gonna make you pay for this," Innocent whispered. "Your days on this earth are limited, you b***h-a** snitch."

Trevor didn't bother to respond to my brother's threats. Instead, he dug into his pocket and pulled out a large knot of money.

"This fool really thinks he can bribe an undercover cop?" Trip questioned. "He's tryin' to get us placed under the jail!"

A big sigh of relief escaped Innocent and Trip when Trevor and the undercover exchanged pleasantries with a handshake, followed by a hug.

"I had y'all both shook, huh?" Trevor asked, while laughing hysterically.

For probably the first time in his life, Innocent found himself speechless. He was unable to do anything but let out a light-hearted chuckle over the prank Trevor had accomplished at his own expense.

"You got me good. So this is your surprise?"

"Yeah," Trevor responded. "This is my partner, Lincoln. Him and I go back way before he decided to cross over and play with the boys in blue. You don't have nothing to worry about. He doesn't even cover this area. He's a Brooklyn pig!"

"You gotta warn a brother before you spring something like this on us, man," Trip advised.

"Man, I ain't gotta tell you nothing! I don't hear your boss complaining. You're lucky I even allow you to listen in on this transaction. So, do me a favor and play the background!"

Lincoln briefly went over his credentials and reminded Trevor that his services didn't come cheap. Even though he was his main connect, he knew full well that he was risking not only his job security, but his freedom also if he were to ever get busted dealing with the ones he had sworn to uphold the law against.

Not one to stand around idly while another man steals his show, Innocent interrupted Lincoln to get his point across.

"So let me understand this. Payment is expected once a month? On the third, right? Five thousand will be left in an envelope that reads 'RENT' in the mailbox of 1234 St. James Place, Apartment 3-A?"

Innocent had a habit of repeating what someone said to him. That was his way of mentally documenting the conversation and giving the other person an opportunity to correct him in the unlikely event he missed anything.

"That's correct," Lincoln responded. "Three p.m. on the dot. Whoever you send can't be late, and it has to be the same person. I won't collect if it's not a recognizable face doing the drop. Understand me?"

"Yeah, I understand. You're not dealing with any rookies."

"So then, we're all in agreement, right?" Trevor questioned. "Lincoln is gonna keep some of the heat from off of us and give us a heads-up when a bust is coming down. He's also gonna shake up some of our competition and keep them from trying to set up shop in our main areas of work."

"You're making me nervous. Why do you keep looking around?" Lincoln asked, staring directly at Trip.

"'Cause I don't trust cops. I don't trust any kind of cop. Ex-cop. Undercover cop. Especially a crooked cop! They're the worse kind of cop. How do we know you're not gonna set us up? Or try to extort us by doubling your fee?"

What happened next was straight out of an action movie. Trevor reached into his jacket, pulled out an automatic, and aimed it in the direction of Trip. To his credit, Trip didn't back down the slightest bit. Instead, he puffed out his chest, daring Trevor to pull the trigger.

"You gonna shoot me? Then go ahead and shoot me mutha*****! Handle your business!"

"You're gonna need to recruit another yes man," Trevor said to Innocent.

"Ain't nobody shooting nobody. Not on my watch!" Innocent proclaimed. "Trevor, put the gun away. You're in the middle of Harlem of all places. So, chill out! Whether you like it or not, we're all family here. Trip is my man from day one, so if you shoot him, then you and I got beef. That's my word."

Trevor took a moment to take in Innocent's remarks and then did as instructed. He slowly lowered his automatic, adjusted the safety, and placed it back into his jacket. Trip, sensing he won the battle, smirked and walked slowly back to Innocent's new Range, where he made himself comfortable in the passenger seat.

Back at Innocent's crib, even a blind man could see that my brother took pride in his surroundings. Since *Scarface* was his all-time favorite movie, he had managed to pattern many of the similarities. Innocent had piranha in a huge fish tank in the dining room, a pool table in his basement, and pictures of slain drug lords throughout the living room. He even went as far as to install a large flat-screen television in his bathroom so he could watch television while soaking in his tub.

"Sometimes you need to stay humble, even when your instincts tell you to do otherwise," Innocent explained.

Trip was actually listening, and every now and then, he nodded his head in agreement. Trip had never intentionally second-guessed any of Innocent's directives and had committed himself to knowing his role as his immediate backup and right-hand man. He would go as far as risking his life for my brother. Anything to stay in his good graces.

"So who are you gonna get to do the drop?" Trip questioned. "You know, the monthly drop off to St. James Place?"

"I don't know. Haven't really thought about it. Why?"

"I'll do it. My grandmom lives up the block from there…a few buildings down from that address. That will give me a chance to check up on her and make sure she's taking her medication."

David L.

"Okay. You got it."

"Don't worry. I'm gonna hold things down over there for you."

"Just try not to be so explosive all the time. Take it easy."

"What do you mean?"

"I mean, you need to learn the art of humility."

"To tell you the truth, I don't even know what humility means."

Before Innocent had the opportunity to give his friend and partner in crime a vocabulary lesson, Crystal, his son's mother, interrupted.

"Your son has been waiting up in his room for over an hour for you to tuck him in. When are you gonna wrap this up?"

Don't get it twisted. My brother was the man in every sense of the word, but Crystal was the woman behind the man. She knew how to get under his skin, and she almost always got her way. Innocent's reasoning was that since he was the king of his castle, he had no choice but to allow his woman to be by his side as his counterpart – a queen.

He responded with his usual laid-back demeanor.

"Alright. Alright. Tell T.J. I'll be in there in a few minutes. I'm finishing up right now."

"No, you tell him, Trent! I'm going to bed."

"Yo, Trip, we can finish this up tomorrow morning."

"What time?"

"Nine."

"In the morning?"

"Did I stutter? Yes, nine in the morning. I'm telling you, Trip...you're slipping. Get your mind right."

"I'll be here. Don't even sweat it."

"Good. Business is good right now, but that doesn't mean we should start getting sloppy. Our competition is up at nine in the morning, so we need to be up at nine in the morning."

"I'll be here by eight fifty-five! Tell little man I said what's up."

30

No matter how many football games I played in, I still got butterflies before the start of one. It was Saturday afternoon, and my team, the Brooklyn Cyclones, was playing the Bronx Grizzlies, an offensively-stacked team. Coach Stevens had it in for me ever since he got word that I was mixing school with football. He didn't think I could do both, and word on the street was that neither did anyone else.

My team made the trip out to the Bronx, and we walked out onto the field to a chorus of boos. The players we were going up against were huge, and at that time of the season, they had not lost a game. That day something had to give because neither had we. The crowd was into this game, as well. A couple of overzealous attendees even went as far as to make signs that read "BROOKLYN SUCKS!" And one fan was yelling obscenities from on top of a fence.

My teammates looked a little nervous with the exception of Big Mike. He was too amped up about the potential NFL scouts that were reportedly dropping by to see him perform. Rumors continued from some of my teammates that Big Mike recently began experimenting with steroids to hopefully increase his chances of getting noticed by some of the local scouts that sometime attended our away games.

My girl Angel had promised to stop by and watch the game, but I didn't see her sitting in the visitor's section anywhere. The crowd became even more animated as, one by one, the Bronx team made their way onto the field. I didn't remember them being that big.

"I hope we get the ball first," one of my teammates said to another. "That way, we can shut down all this damn noise coming from the stands."

He had a point. I heard one year things got so live from up

in the stands that after the game, most of the fans stormed the field and started a fight with some of the opposing players.

Now for the coin toss. We called heads. Yes! We got the ball first! My boy Felix had been given the added assignment of returning on punt returns, as well as being the primary runner coming out of the backfield.

"This is my time to shine," Felix murmured to me, while we ran onto the field.

He was fast enough to get some notice from the scouts that were there that day, but personally, I didn't think he quite had what it took or the football I.Q. needed to go all the way. It was three minutes and thirty-six seconds into the game, and we were up seven to zero. Exactly four plays and less than fifteen yards later the Grizzlies turned the ball over and gave us excellent field position. If we were able to keep our momentum up, that Bronx team would be facing their first loss of the season in about two and a half hours left of game time.

Halftime. We were up by two touchdowns, and I didn't see Angel anywhere in sight. It figured she would miss my best game of the season. In just two quarters of play, Felix had run for one hundred and forty-three yards, and Big Mike had protected our quarterback and allowed zero sacks, which was quite a feat since he had been double-teamed by the defensive line all game. My numbers weren't too shabby either. Four catches for seventy-two yards. Every pass that came my way I caught.

Coach Steven's halftime speeches were getting so repetitive that I could almost recite it word for word.

"We've only played half a game, sissies!" he shouted. "That means there is still half a game left to play!"

Coach Stevens spat whenever he was excited, and his face turned beet red. If he wasn't careful, one day he would blow a blood vessel.

"Is there anyone here who wants to call it quits and lay down and die?" he questioned.

As usual, no one dared to respond, not even Chester, our starting fullback and official clown of the team. Everyone was too focused. You could read the intensity on all of our faces. If we won that game, we claimed the top spot in our division. It was that simple.

As we ran back onto the field, the crowd became even more animated, with some fans throwing empty soda cans at us. They took their football that serious out there. Our Bronx rivals got the ball first and scored on the initial punt return. The score was 14–7. On our first possession since halftime ended, we punted the ball off after only three plays. The momentum had definitely shifted in their favor.

"Get in for Johnson!" Coach Stevens yelled out to one of our special team's players.

Jay Johnson, our starting middle linebacker, had played so poorly up to this point that he would be lucky if he saw the playing field again for the rest of the game. He had missed key tackles, overrun basic plays, and his heart didn't seem to be in the game.

The remaining minutes of the third quarter went by without too much more activity. Score was still 14–7. No one escaped Coach Stevens' wrath as he slapped everyone on their helmets to get his point across. With one more quarter to go, it was do or die time for my Brooklyn Cyclones.

Fourth quarter. For the second straight time, we punted after only three offensive plays. We had become too predictable. Run, run, followed by a screen pass. Next possession: run, run, followed by another screen pass, but this one to the opposite side of the field. The Grizzlies were becoming cocky and playing like true champions. After a desperation timeout called by the coach, we finally got the ball back, and my defender had his eyes locked onto mine.

"Nothing personal, but I'm gonna celebrate after my next takeaway. Tell your QB I said thanks."

"Yeah, whatever," I meagerly responded.

David L.

I didn't like to talk trash during game time. I would rather let my actions on the field overshadow the words that may come out of my mouth. Once again, we got stopped on three plays, but not before I caught another pass for nine yards. I looked my defender in the eyes and chuckled to myself. Win or lose, I was going to get my numbers on that day. After a thirty-six-yard run by the opposing running back, the score was now tied 14-14 with a little less than four minutes left on the clock. There were sounds of grumbling on our side of the field, but no one dared voice their concerns to Coach Stevens.

"I'm giving it all I got, fellas. Y'all need to do your part," Big Mike complained.

"I got a hundred and seventy yards under my belt," Felix responded.

"Yeah, but you haven't produced squat since the beginning of the second half," Big Mike counter-responded.

Those two were like a cat and dog, always trying to one up the other. It began the beginning of the season and never slowed down.

As I looked over into the crowd, I saw a familiar face enter the stands. It was Angel. Like her name, she was a godsend, and I could feel my energy level reach new heights. I had no choice but to show and prove.

"Coach, you gotta put me back in. I can take my guy. No way can he get physical with me off the line of scrimmage."

Coach Stevens was hesitant at first, but eventually gave in to my pleas and placed me in the slot for an across-the-field pass play designed to open up the left- and right-side receivers.

I looked over at Angel once more and then got focused. The play worked as designed, and I got another reception good for fifteen yards. With only a minute left in regulation, I got another reception good for thirteen yards, which put our kicker in excellent position for the game winner. To make a long story short, he kicked it straight through the goal post. Final score was 17–14, and we remained undefeated just as I privately predicted.

There were at least three hundred people yelling in the stands, but I could only hear one lone voice cheering me on for my brilliant playmaking. Say what you want about me. Right at that exact moment, I was the man. Ask anybody if you don't take my word for it!

CHAPTER THREE

The corner of Nostrand and Gates Avenue was usually a hot spot. However, that day was somehow different. Innocent rolled up in his spanking new 2010 Range Rover with his handpicked entourage driving behind him. At times, he did this more for show than anything else. As usual, Trip was riding shotgun and going through Innocent's IPod looking for a song to play that met his taste.

"Do I make a left right here?" Innocent questioned.

"Yeah, right here," Trip responded.

"You sure? Right here?"

That's my brother Innocent...always repeating himself.

"Yo, Innocent, you're strapped, right?"

"I keep a piece on me at all times. Why? You got beef out here that I don't know about?"

"Nah, nothing like that, but there's a lot of jealousy over in these parts. We're making money... a lot of money. That's gotta stir up some enemies and some ill feelings, don't cha think?"

"You worry too much. I've been runnin' these streets my entire life. It's all about respect. No matter what you do, you're gonna have at least a minimum of enemies waiting for your downfall. You know how the song goes…more money, more problems. Jealousy is from anyone waiting for you to fall flat on your face, but my respect will always be demanded. That's how I do."

Innocent's Range Rover was now parked in front of a hydrant on the corner of a dead-end street in the Fort Greene section of Brooklyn. My brother's swagger was obvious as he got out with Trip and walked into what looked like an abandoned building. Both Innocent and Trip flinched when a large rat scurried past them and entered a small hole in the corner of the first-floor stairwell. For all of their machismo and bravado, they both reacted like straight b*****s at the sight of a harmless rodent.

Two individuals wearing black hoodies and Timberland boots made their presence known. It was never like my brother to be doing nickel-and-dime street business, so there must have been something special about this particular meeting…and there was.

The two hooded individuals were "Lord" and "Wise." Their status was very similar to my brother and Trip. Lord was the "HNIC" of a drug ring in his area, and Wise was his deputy. Lord's crew ran deep…an army of at least twenty drug runners and gun slingers, and those numbers were continuing to grow at an alarming rate. Innocent didn't have as large an army as Lord, but financially, he had no equal. He knew it, too, and had no problem reminding people when they got out of line.

"I didn't think you were gonna show up," Lord declared.

He had a smug smile on his face, as did Wise. Neither had any hesitancy to test the limits of my brother and Trip, especially since both happened to be out of their immediate safety net in this particular part of Brooklyn.

"Why wouldn't I?" Innocent responded. "I'm a legend in these parts. They love me out here!"

"So then, let's get down to business."

Everyone was now seated at a large, round table in an

apartment furnished with nothing more than a few lopsided chairs, a plaid living room couch, and a ripped-up stuffed teddy bear lying dormant in a corner of the room. If you looked close enough, you could detect that the teddy bear had an eye missing. Quite possibly a camera was placed where the eye used to be, and that harmless "stuffed animal" was really doubling as a video camera aimed to set up Innocent and Trip for the cops.

"So what's it gonna be? Give us the whole other side of Atlantic Avenue up to Utica and we'll call it even. Whatcha think?" Lord questioned.

Lord had his hand on a map, while taking a pull of his Marlboro cigarette for emphasis.

"I think you're crazy," Innocent responded. "You already have from Classon Avenue all the way down to Pacific. Not to mention you own the Flatbush Avenue strip, the majority of Fort Greene…hell, you even got connects over by Fulton!"

Innocent and Lord negotiated back and forth, while their respective "deputies" listened in attentively. Neither dared say anything, instead preferring to every now and then nod their heads in apparent agreement to what their respective boss was saying.

"Why don't we break bread over a bottle?" Lord challenged.

On cue, Wise got up from his chair and pulled a bottle of Grey Goose Vodka from a cabinet in the kitchen.

"Nah, I'm good," Innocent responded. "And what's up with this place? You're making serious money now. Step your game up!"

"I do most of my business here in this rundown place. The pigs already think that all we do is make money to immediately run out and buy flashy cars and walk around with thousands of dollars' worth of jewelry on. That's why can't none of us stay out of jail. 'Cause we're all so easy to spot."

"You may have a point," Innocent replied. "At the same time, you have to live life. We all only got one life, right?"

"I respect that," Lord said. "But, we're all making crazy

money out here. Right now as I speak, I'm donating money to the Boys & Girls Club not too far from here. Anything to take care of these little soldiers runnin' through these streets!'"

Who said a major drug lord couldn't have a soft heart and meaningful intentions?

Innocent and Lord shook hands and promised to reconvene at a later date. No bad blood. No beef. Just the way it was supposed to go down in the hood between two powerful bosses. All in all, it was a good day.

On the way out of the building, Innocent handed a kid, who was no older than twelve and riding a busted-up bike, a twenty dollar bill for no reason. Maybe he was inspired by Lord's little speech. He was all smiles until he walked up to his Range Rover and found that he had gotten a ticket for parking too close to a fire hydrant. As expected, he balled the ticket up and tossed it into a nearby garbage can. No license. No worries.

I was still hung over from drinking too much and recovering from New Year's Day. That also meant that in about two weeks, I would be going into my last semester of school. Not too much to complain about. I was able to hold down a "B" average, have a beautiful woman for a girlfriend, and my Brooklyn Cyclones team was in the playoffs for the first time in franchise history. The lingering remnants of Hennessey could be tasted in my mouth and the stench of cigar smoke was on my clothes. I must've really been trashed, because I went to sleep fully dressed. Something I never did. I had recently given Angel a key to my apartment, and I could hear her using it for the first time to let herself in.

"I'm in the bedroom," I yelled out.

"Take two of these," she said, while handing me some Advil

for my throbbing head.

I got the usual lecture about overdoing it when hanging out with the fellas, more specifically my boys Swift and Tone. I also got the obligatory and stern warning about drinking and driving, even though I was in my apartment the entire time. It didn't help my case when I jokingly responded that I drive better when under the influence.

"It's my day off. I want to go out and eat," Angel said.

My facial grimace gave me away, but reluctantly, I got out of bed and hit the shower. Minutes later, I was drying off, while at the same time looking through my PalmPilot for a good place to eat.

"What are you in the mood for?" I asked.

"Seafood. I have a craving for the Surf 'n Turf over at Red Lobster."

"Damn, girl! The closest one is in Sheepshead Bay."

"And? That's what I'm in the mood for."

I grudgingly finished getting dressed and pulled out my last fifty-dollar bill from my dresser drawer. The ride there wasn't too bad and traffic was at a minimum. Although there were still signs of last week's snowstorm on the pavement, I had the window down as I tried to shake my hangover from the night before. The downside to that was listening to Angel as she complained about how cold it was in the car.

I could envision myself biting into one of those delicious biscuits Red Lobster was so famous for. Unfortunately for me, my appetite would have to wait, as we were told that there would be a minimum of a forty-five minute to an hour wait before we could be seated.

Halfway through our meal, a familiar face could be seen from a distance. Innocent's woman Crystal and a bunch of her crew came waltzing in and literally walked right to a table. No wait. Nothing. They were all very loud and dressed like they just came from the club. The wrong glance from any patron in their immediate vicinity could possibly result in a straight-up beatdown. My brother's reputation was in full effect as two workers walked over from the bar area and placed a bucket full of Corona beers on their table. It took a few moments, but Crystal finally recognized me and motioned me over. By then, Angel was done with her meal and so was I, and we were just waiting for the check.

"So what's going on, little *brother-in-law*? What brings you up in here?" Crystal questioned.

She thought she was slick. Privately, Crystal was fuming that Innocent had never proposed to her. Until he did, she was nothing more than a glorified baby's mama and she knew it. I responded as tactfully as only I could, keeping in mind that not once did Crystal acknowledge my girl Angel standing next to me.

"I'm doing good. Just came out to get a bite to eat real quick."

"He's kinda cute," one of Crystal's girls said to another friend at the table.

She wasn't totally indiscreet about her impromptu comment either. Instead, it was a daring combination of quiet enough to get a few well-placed giggles from everyone at the table, yet loud enough for Angel to hear and walk out of the restaurant and over to the car.

"Your friend is not a people person, huh?" Crystal asked.

I wanted to say she was, but not when she's around ignorant, ghetto-a** chicks. However, I wisely declined and used my better judgment instead.

"She's not feeling too well. Stomach cramps or something," I responded.

I instinctively knew I was going to get it from Angel when I got to the car, so I made my exit from Crystal and her crew immediately.

"See you later, little brother," she said, as I quickly raced to where Angel was waiting for me.

She was already in the passenger seat and the music was

blaring from the new speakers I had installed. A telltale sign she was pissed off.

"Take me home," she vehemently said.

Yep, a telltale sign. It was going to be a helluva evening.

I had six messages waiting for me upon my return to my apartment. They were all from my brother – each more scattered than the one before it. He wanted me to take a ride with him out to Philadelphia and watch his back while he took care of business there. He had been trying to get me in on the family business for a couple of years. I had always told him no, and that day was no different. I called him back fully expecting an argument of some sort.

"You need to stop being such a b***h and take this ride with me," Innocent said loudly over the phone.

"You know I can't get caught up in your mess. I got school to think about."

"School? You can't be serious, little brother. You hang with me and you can buy your own school! That's for real. At least start slowly and do a couple of out-of-town runs in one of the trucks. We got six of them now. You can report to work tomorrow morning, and I'll have Trip walk you through everything you need to do."

"I'm in school, so I don't have to drive a truck for a living. Besides, if I ever got pulled over driving one of them trucks, that would be it for me. No thanks!"

He had his opinion and I had mine, and it looked like neither of us was going to budge. I clicked over and my sister Tammy was on the other end. I promptly hung up with Innocent only to get the same nonsense from her.

"You really need to think about it," she said matter-of-factly. "You can stand to make a whole lot of money from one trip with Innocent. You could buy that school you're going to!"

No wonder Innocent and Tammy were so damn close. They thought alike and acted alike. It was like they were the same person. Now my cell phone was blowing up. First, I received a call from Tone telling me to meet up with him at Sammy's later that evening. Sammy's was a hole-in-the-wall bar that was frequented back in the day. I hadn't been to that spot in well over a year. I told Tone that I would meet up with him around ten o'clock. My phone call with him was followed by a text from my boy Swift telling me the same thing – to come out to Sammy's later on that night. What was going on at Sammy's that night that both Tone and Swift were trying to get me to come down? I figured I might as well try to get some shut eye, because it looked like it was going to be one of those nights. Before I did, I had to call Angel so we could make up.

Swift offered to pick me up on his way to Tone's apartment, so I graciously obliged. I wasn't going to pass up a chance to save money, especially with the way gas prices were on the rise. From Tone's, the ride to Sammy's was about a fifteen- to twenty-minute drive. Of course, we had to get there first without any incidents.

"Yo, Swift, we got company," I said, making sure my seatbelt was fastened.

The company I was referring to was five-0 who had just put on their sirens and was now motioning us to pull the car over. For whatever reason, Swift briefly hesitated, then complied and sat idly in the driver's seat, prepared for whatever was to happen next. It was a tense moment in time as the police officer took his time getting out of his squad car, almost as if he was baiting us to get out before him and make a run for it.

"He must be checking my plate," Swift said to me.

He was trying to remain as calm as possible, but I could tell he was slightly flustered. If this was a prelude for the rest of the night, my immediate thought was to turn around and go back home before anything else happened.

"License and registration," the officer said in a commanding voice.

"What's the problem, officer?" Swift questioned.

I stayed silent, opting to see what happened next. Swift was driving his woman's car, so I knew it was legit. Plus, he was already on probation for an assault charge that he went down for the previous year. So, I knew he wouldn't be stupid enough to be in possession of anything illegal.

The officer, and now his partner who just made his way out of another patrol car that had pulled up, walked back over to us after a few moments of making us wait.

"You are good to go," the officer remarked.

"You never told me why you pulled me over in the first place," Swift responded.

It was at that exact moment I knew we were going to get it. I gave Swift that signature "look" of mine. The one that said "Shut the hell up before we end up in jail."

"I would suggest you drive off while you're ahead," the officer warned.

"Don't think I can't read a badge number," Swift replied.

Everything afterwards was like a blur. I had a feeling from the time those sirens came on that there was going to be a problem. We were in the middle of Brighton Beach with nothing but White folks that didn't like us in their neighborhood, and I was being motioned by five-0 to get out of the car. Swift was being detained in the back seat of the patrol car, and neither of us knew why. Maybe we got pulled over for DWB – Driving While Black!

"We're taking your friend with the smart mouth down to the station for questioning," the officer said to me. "His car is going to eventually be towed, so I strongly suggest you find another way to get to wherever you're heading. Enjoy the rest of your night."

I watched in disbelief as Swift was driven off, still running his mouth from the back seat of the patrol car.

I was at the Old Country Diner waiting for Tone to come pick me up so we could head over to the police station and get Swift. With the exception of a couple of Black waitresses, I was the only other Black individual in the whole joint. I was beginning to get that feeling of déjà vu. The prejudice level was at an all-time high as three waitresses walked directly by me without the faintest hint of attention. The diner had a bar section, so I headed over to get a drink before Tone arrived. Over at the bar was no different. Two older guys got their drinks before me, even though I was already at the bar waiting.

"Am I invisible?" I questioned.

"I'll be over in a minute," the bartender responded.

That minute turned into another minute...followed by five more minutes. Way too long for a drink that was probably going to be watered down anyway. The bartender finally made his way over to me, but by then, I was no longer interested in anything from him or the diner he worked for.

"I guess I'm not your type to get a drink like everyone else, huh? My money is green just like everyone else's up in here," I said.

My comment was loud enough to get a bunch of random looks from some of the bartender's more loyal patrons. Loud enough for the manager to walk over and add his "two cents".

"What seems to be the problem, lad?" he asked.

That's when I knew I wasn't imagining anything. That "lad" comment was straight out of a Roots mini-series!

"I'm a grown-a** man!" I responded. "And I don't like the service up in here!"

"Well then, I suggest you take your business elsewhere."

I was momentarily at a loss for words. Not because I was intimidated by the bar manager, but because almost every single person within listening distance was of the Caucasian persuasion. I finally got the nerve to offer my rebuttal.

"I'm leaving. Not because you said so, but because I know if I were to order a drink, someone would probably piss in it, you racist scumbag!"

More random stares were upon me as I made my way out of the diner. Within moments of waiting for Tone at the corner, he pulled up to the curb and beeped the horn, signaling his need for attention.

"Yo, those are some racist bastards up in there!" I said, while pointing over to the diner as we drove by.

"What do you expect?" Tone replied. "We're up in Brighton Beach. You think you in Fort Greene or something?"

"I should've smacked that damn racist bastard up in there!"

"You wanna go back there and handle your business?"

Tone called my bluff with precision. So, instead, I reminded him that we had more pressing concerns to handle.

After he programmed his navigation system, we pulled up to the police station in less than three minutes. As soon as we entered, all eyes were on us. Swift was filling out paperwork at the front desk. He was never formally charged with anything, so the process did not take long at all. The local strong arm of the law just felt like messing with him – and it worked. I'm sure Swift walked into the precinct hollering at the top of his lungs. Now that he had been humbled, he was the complete opposite. At least in front of the boys in blue, he remained calm.

We took a vote and none of us were any longer in the mood to continue on our original destination to Sammy's. Could you blame us?

CHAPTER FOUR

"**Y**o, Innocent, what time is your pops supposed to show up?" Trip asked.

"He'll be here shortly. Relax. When have you known him to be late for anything?"

My brother and Trip were seated in a northeast section of the Bronx. It was a prearranged compromise since Innocent and his team still resided in Brooklyn and my pops lived in Connecticut. They met monthly at the same pool hall my pops used to always play pool at and run numbers out of before his relocation to Greenwich, Connecticut.

"Here he comes now," Innocent declared. "I see him pulling up at the corner."

Not unexpectedly, Crime waltzed into the pool hall with his usual swagger and grace. Behind him was what looked to be a mid-twenty-year-old White woman who could've easily doubled as a beauty pageant finalist. She was wearing a full-length mink coat and her blonde hair was blowing in every conceivable direction. The pool hall consisted of mainly men, and every one of them tried to be as nonchalant as possible as they made eye contact with the mystery woman.

"Can I get a tab going over here?" Crime said, looking over at the waitress standing in front of him. "So how's business?" he questioned.

"I'm holding the fort down like always," Innocent replied. "I'm looking to take over a couple of blocks over on Nostrand. Shouldn't take too long to finalize the deal."

"What about the competition? You're gonna have the cops coming down hard. The same ones you send packin' are gonna retaliate by sending the boys in blue for you, that's for sure. You ready for that type of attention?"

"Yeah, I know. My boy Trip here has a lookout crew that's over ten deep. We'll be alright."

"Yeah, Crime, I got this. You got nothing to worry about," Trip interrupted.

Crime motioned to a patron to imply he had next on the pool table. While he racked the table, he continued to receive random stares from the low-level thugs and female patrons. His strong will and aura had taken time to get to the point where it was, and he took his legendary status seriously up in the pool hall.

Trip and my brother motioned to the waitress and ordered Buffalo wings and nachos. Both knew real business was not going to be discussed until Crime got in at least a couple of games. One by one, Crime sent his victims back to the bar to make change for another shot at his pool title. During one game, his opponent didn't even get a chance to take a shot.

"Alright, boys, I'm done playing pool for the day. There's no competition for me here anyway. Let's get down to business."

Not one to stay in one place for too long, Crime instructed Trip and Innocent to follow him and his lady friend to a nearby Sprint store. It was in a heavily populated section of the Bronx, and both my pops and Innocent were forced to double-park due to the congested traffic.

"Why are we here in front of this Sprint store?" Innocent questioned.

"Because you need to start getting into the habit of changing your cell phone carrier every so often. The boys in blue and the Feds can track all of your conversations when you don't switch up your phones," Crime responded.

Right on cue, one of Crime's workers walked up to everyone as they remained huddled outside of the Sprint store. He had a noticeable limp, thin frame, and was sporting a very outdated pair of Jordan sneakers.

"Fellas, this is Craig. He also goes by 'C'. Whenever you need to switch phones, he's your man. You call him on this number and hook up right here. Every time and day that you meet will always be different from the last."

Crime proceeded to pull out a business card and hand it to my brother.

"Put this in a safe place. Today is Friday, and the time is six o'clock p.m., right? That means the next time y'all hook up, it will be on a Saturday at seven o'clock p.m. After that, your next meeting will be on a Sunday, and the time will be eight o'clock p.m. Does everyone understand the arrangement?"

Everyone nodded their head in agreement. Well, everyone except Trip. As usual, he felt it necessary to add his quirky comments to the meet up.

"What if the next meeting falls on a holiday? What about five or six meetings from now? The time we meet would be like two o'clock in the morning. Who wants to meet up in front of a closed Sprint store at two o'clock in the morning?"

He did have a point, but no one dared go against my father's reasoning. He was quickly silenced by my brother and instructed to walk around the corner to check on both cars that were double-parked. C walked into the Sprint store to handle his business with the store manager and make the cell phone arrangement for everyone. Trip immediately returned with a perplexed look on his face and an envelope in his hand.

"What's up?" Innocent asked. "Don't tell me I got another ticket."

"I don't think it's a ticket. It's got your name on it. You better open it."

Innocent immediately took the envelope from Trip and opened it with anticipation, while my pops looked on with suspense. The seconds literally felt like hours. Both hands were now clenched as Innocent took the letter and passed it to Crime to read. He was looking up toward the sky, as if the answer to his many questions were up there in full view.

"Yo, Innocent, what does it say? Don't keep me in the dark," Trip said.

"NO! This has to be a bluff!" Crime responded, referring to the letter that read: While You're Out There Playing GOD, I'm At Your House Right Now Playing With Your Son And Getting Ready To Have My Way With Your Old Lady!

Angel and I awakened from our routine evening nap to the frantic rants of my sister Tammy, who ordered me out of the bed and instructed me to immediately head over to my brother's house. I lived the closest to him, and according to her, time was of the essence.

"What's goin' on? What's so important that I have to leave my warm apartment and go out in this cold-a** weather?" I grumbled.

"Just get over to Innocent's house right this minute and don't argue with me! I'll meet you over there in about twenty minutes."

"Where is Innocent? Did something happen to him?"

"He's stuck in the Bronx with pops. Someone did a number to both of their cars. Their tires were flattened. Now get ya a** over to the house!"

Angel and I argued for several minutes as we got dressed.

She wanted to tagalong, and I proclaimed that I was putting my foot down and that she couldn't go. Guess who won that battle!

"Call your brother's house," Angel commanded.

"I did already. No one picked up."

The ride there was very tense, and a knot was swelling in the pit of my stomach. With all the dirt my brother had done throughout the years, had someone or something finally caught up to him? I would know the answer to that question shortly thereafter, as I raced up to his semi-gated community.

It was very conservative and mostly inhabited by retired White couples that probably despised Blacks in their neighborhood, even those with money that could afford to reside there. It was a good thing my cell phone was on its charger, because I was literally averaging a phone call every thirty seconds. Innocent followed by Trevor, our old family contact who couldn't make it down because he was out in Virginia taking care of business, and then my sister followed once more by Innocent.

When I pulled up to the corner, Angel and I gasped. There was fire trucks and police cars parked on the lawn. Crystal was holding little T.J. in her arms as a police officer took a report from her. I was greeted by a hug.

"Who did this?" I questioned.

Crystal was noticeably quieter, so I reasoned there was much more to the story than what I was led to assume. Moments later, my always emotional sister pulled up to all of the commotion.

"We're gonna get the mutha****** that did this to your house!" she screamed at the top of her lungs.

"Shhh! Chill, Tammy," Crystal told her. "Now isn't the time or place for all of that. All that matters right this moment is no one was hurt and the fire department was able to get here in time to save the house and everything in it."

After the fire department had put the fire completely out and the police did their job, they all eventually left, but not before more note writing and interviewing.

"We'll be in touch," one of the firemen announced. He then proceeded to hand Crystal a phone number written on a sheet of paper for her to keep in contact with him.

While awaiting my brother's arrival, we all gathered on the front porch, viewing the burnt remnants of the screen door. After a two and a half hour wait for Triple A, Innocent and Trip pulled up to the house. They were followed by my pops and his lady friend. Some of the neighbors that resided in the nearby houses had come through to offer their support. Either that or they were just being nosy.

"Don't worry. I'm gonna get the mutha****** that did this," Innocent whispered to Crystal, who was now back outside along with the rest of us.

As usual, Tammy continued to rant and rave, and had to be reminded by my pops that she was in the company of White folk and needed to keep her voice down. Truth be told, the only one that didn't stand out on this chilly night was my pop's lady friend, who was still sitting in his ride.

"Take T.J. back into the house. It's too cold for him to be out here," Innocent said to Crystal. "I'll be inside shortly."

With fists clenched and a vein bulging from the side of his forehead, Innocent was beside himself. He was used to dishing out pain and suffering, not being on the receiving end of it. With the envelope in his hand, Innocent went in behind Crystal to inform her of what transpired earlier and to get additional information about the fire. He quickly returned and informed the rest of us what was in the letter and how he had just been told by Crystal that one of the neighbors witnessed a black sedan with tinted windows stop in front of the house. Then he went into detail about how two large Black men walked onto the porch and placed something in the mail slot, which led into the outer hallway of the house.

"It's all beginning to make sense," Crime blurted out.

Everyone listened attentively to hear what he had to say

next.

"Their plan was probably to get Crystal and T.J. out of the house and abduct them. They must've been prematurely scared off by something…or someone. Trip, I want you to make sure that under no circumstances is Crystal and T.J. left alone. When I'm not here, I need you to take control and stay in the basement. I need you, too, Prentice."

"Me? What can I do?"

"I want you to stay in the guest room. I have to go down to Philly tomorrow, so pack some clothes and hold me down until I get back. Can you do that?"

"Yeah, sure, I got you, I suppose. Don't worry about a thing."

"You got company," Crime said, motioning to a neighbor walking over in our direction.

"I saw everything that went down," the man said.

He was the only other Black person that lived on the block besides his wife and infant child.

"I didn't want to say anything in front of the cops, but I saw when the two men pulled up in front of your house. I was watching closely because they circled the block about three times. Every time they drove up to your house, their car slowed down more and more."

"Did you see their faces?" Crime questioned.

"No, I didn't, but they lit something and tossed it into the mail slot. They didn't drive off right away. Not until I came out and turned my front porch light on. I think the light scared them off."

"Damn. So you didn't see either one of them, huh?" Tammy murmured.

"No, but I have something better than that. I have their license plate number."

He proceeded to reach into his pocket and hand my brother a license plate number written on a napkin. Then he started walking back over to his house.

David L.

After promising to keep in close contact with one another, we all dispersed so that Innocent could get back inside to his woman and child – but not before Crime walked over to the man before he could get into his house and handed him five one-hundred-dollar bills in a money clip for his information.

To say my relationship with Angel had been strained since I began staying at my brother's house would be a serious understatement. She and I had been bickering over the most minor things, and somehow, she thought she was losing me to the streets and to my family.

"How long do you have to be here anyway?" Angel asked.

"Shhh! Crystal will hear you from upstairs. Relax. My brother will be back home in a couple of days."

"He better be. And what about Tammy and your father? How come they're not here watching over Crystal and your nephew?"

"Because they're out handling business."

"And what does that mean?"

"Look, girl, I don't know. Just trust me on this. Go on home, and I'll catch up with you later."

Innocent's phone had been ringing non-stop since the morning after the fire, but I was instructed, as was Crystal, not to answer it unless we recognized the caller. Usually, the unknown caller would let the phone ring and then hang up before leaving a message. There was one time the person on the other end had a change in plans.

"You tell Innocent he's a dead mutha****** and that his girl is one dead b***h! Last time was just a warning. Next time, we're gonna show you we mean business! That's on my life!"

I immediately played the message back to Crystal and sent

Innocent a text message. I also sent my pops a text message – followed by one to Tammy. My pops was the first to respond and instructed me to contact his old running mate, Trevor. He had just returned from a Virginia contract a few hours beforehand, and with little to no hours of sleep, he left his Long Island home to meet up with Crystal and me at Innocent's crib.

Trevor pulled up into Innocent's driveway driving a brand-new 2010 Cadillac Escalade. Typical old head, hood n***a that still thought he was twenty-five. With everything he had been taught about being too flashy, he still overdid everything, from the car he drove to the clothes he wore on his back. I didn't notice at first, but the entire time Trevor was in her house, Crystal looked at him with apprehension. If I didn't know better, I would think she didn't care too much for him.

"Let me hear the message," he said to the lady of the house.

Crystal obliged and played the message back. He was tapping his feet on the ground and biting his lower lip, a telltale sign that usually meant he was in deep thought. A few moments later, Tammy arrived at the house and asked to hear the recording. Again, Crystal obliged.

"I don't feel safe at all, and I can't put my son in this type of danger," Crystal said hysterically.

Tammy was equally as frantic and was pacing all over the living room area. Little T.J. was running around the house, totally oblivious to the possible perils that awaited him.

"Where's Pops?" Tammy asked.

I told her that I left him a text message and reminded her that because of his previous dealings with the law throughout Brooklyn, he was not exactly the most welcome face.

"I have a visitor's wing at my house, Crystal. You and Lil' Innocent are welcome to stay there if you like," Trevor said.

Crystal politely turned down Trevor's offer and went to check on my nephew who was now calling out for his mommy.

"So what are we gonna do?" I questioned.

"We're not gonna do anything…not yet anyway. They want

us to react....show emotion...get sloppy. We're better than that. No. For now, we're just gonna lay low and chill. That is, until Innocent gets back."

When my pops showed up to the house, on his command, we each decided to wait it out for a few more hours, except for Tammy who received a call from her loser boyfriend to come back home. I couldn't hear the entire conversation, but it had something to do with him getting a boot placed on his car. Knowing him, it was probably a result of him owing on his child support payments from a previous relationship.

Just as things began to quiet down in the house, and Crystal stopped her hysterics, the phone rang once more. This time, there would be no recorded message as my pops picked up the receiver and placed the caller on speakerphone.

"Who is this?" Crime questioned.

"This is the person that's going to kill that mutha****** Innocent, then his girl, and maybe you, as well!"

"Well, I tell you what then. Why don't you give me your address so I can come over and make it easier for you?"

"Nah, that's okay. I think I'll begin with Innocent. Is this his father talking? Big, bad Forrester Mitchell? Yeah, I know your full government name, Forrester! On second thought, maybe I'll begin with you!"

Click.

After the unknown voice hung up the phone, everyone looked in unison at my pops to see what he would do or say next.

"Yo, Trevor, find out when Innocent is coming back to Brooklyn. We're in for a war!"

CHAPTER FIVE

T alk about a bad week. I was behind in all of my classes and nowhere close to completion on any of my papers for school. I missed that afternoon's practice, and my coach would make me pay for it when we played later that week. And to top it all off, Angel was still not talking to me. That means no a** anytime soon. Anyone who ever said that peer pressure wasn't a b***h never lived life in my shoes.

"Yo, P, you need to take this ride with us."

"Yeah, kid. We got s**t on lock over where we at. You won't even have to touch the stuff. We got runners that handle the merchandise for us."

Those voices belonged to none other than Tone and Swift, who were trying to get me to get down with their little hustling crew. Little did they know their self-proclaimed "empire" was nothing more than a nickel-and-dime circus compared to what my brother had managed to put together throughout the last couple of years. I hadn't buckled under the pressure to work for a pro league, so why join their amateur team?

"How far can you really go on a college degree anyway? The White man ain't tryin' to pay you top dollar for all your blood, sweat, and tears!" Tone commented.

He had always been big on comparing everything to the White man's stronghold on Black America. He was an ex-Five Percenter who still tried to preach to whoever would listen. Sounds kinda hypocritical coming from a man pumping poison into his own community. A man who would sell dope to his own family members – and reportedly had in the past! Swift, on the other hand, had been the same grimy, stick-you-with-a-rusty-fork type of dude he had been from the moment I met him. He had been dealing dope from the time he was in junior high school and quit school altogether by the time he entered the eleventh grade. He had been doing dirt for so long that he took pride in watching others go down the same path he had gone down throughout the years.

"Yo, come take this ride with us," Swift insisted.

To this day, I don't know the reason why, but I was intrigued. Maybe it was the fast lifestyle that lured me into at least considering to get in the car with them.

"Where to?" I responded.

"Damn, man. Stop asking so many questions!"

"Yeah, man. You act like you better than us or something. It's like that?"

"Nah, nuttin' like that, but I have to run over to my girl's place. I promised her that I'd run some errands for her while her family is in town visiting."

"Alright then. Come on and take this ride. We'll have you back in plenty of time…promise."

Like I said before, peer pressure is a b***h, but nonetheless, I hopped into Tone's ride and privately hoped for the best.

The three of us rolled up to the Cliff Duncan projects over on the south side of the Bronx. I'm still not quite sure why we had to leave our comfort zone of Brooklyn, but that was where we ended up. Although it had to be at least thirty degrees outside that night, there were stick-up kids and young girls out with their babies hanging in front of every corner bodega that we drove by. I never was quite at ease about the whole situation, but I figured Tone and Swift had everything under control. They supposedly made a drop off there once a month and dealt with a couple of clientele that they have had on their payroll for well over a year.

"That's Chico right over there!" Tone yelled, while rolling down his window to get the guy's attention.

Chico was not really his name, but the nickname fit him. As Tone explained it, the Hispanic guy that walked over to the car looked like a person whose name should be Chico.

"Where are Maseo and Rasta?" Swift questioned.

"Maseo got picked up by undercover three nights ago during a sting, and Rasta left town shortly afterwards. They got a warrant out for his arrest," Chico responded.

As Chico explained it, one of his boys was detained and the other – running from the long arm of the law. He must have known that he was on their radar, as well.

Now I was getting a little anxious. As cash and product exchanged hands, I kept my eyes glued for undercover just in case I had to make a run for it. Across the street at a local bodega, more illegal activity was going down as an unassuming teen walked by and placed a small package into a woman's baby stroller. I saw what looked to be a prostitute get into a blue Ford Explorer directly in front of us. The truck had tinted windows, but I could see movement from the back seat. What happened to the days when people went to their local roach motel to get their rocks off?

"One hundred dollars is missing from this stash," Tone said candidly.

"Let me count it again," Chico responded.

He did just that, and upon catching the error, he apologized and went into his back pocket to make up the difference. Maybe it was me, but Tone and Swift's contact seemed to have been stalling. He kept staring through the side view mirror like he was waiting for someone else to arrive. I finally decided to exit the car and head across the street to a nearby Chinese takeout spot. I hadn't eaten in several hours, so I was feeling irritable. The way their boy was stalling, I would be back with my order of shrimp fried rice in plenty of time.

After my food was handed to me, I pulled out a five spot to pay the lady who barely made eye contact with me the entire time I was in her establishment. I guess according to her, we all looked the same anyway.

Just as I started walking over to Tone's car, I saw lights and heard the ominous sounds of police sirens. Sure enough, two cop cars rolled up to Tone's ride — one directly behind him and the other in front of him. Their reaction was instantaneous.

"Yo, P, get the hell outta here!" Swift said, who was first to take off running.

Tone and Chico were right behind him, as they quickly separated to make the chase that much more interesting. My jaw dropped from awe, and my Chinese food dropped onto the cold pavement as I began running in the opposite direction. Looking over my shoulder, I noticed one cop had gotten out of his squad car and was chasing me on foot. I was privately praying that the law of averages was on my side tonight. There were a total of two cops and four of us. That should have made the odds more in our favor. Except for one thing…two more squad cars pulled up and attempted to surround me and Chico. It was now every man for himself. Chico seemed to be ignored, and instead, they directed their attention to me. It must've been a set up. Maybe they weren't giving him as much attention because he was the one that tipped them off.

It was beginning to make much more sense now. He conveniently left out the part of his story earlier about the fact that he probably got picked up, as well, and was granted leniency if he squealed. Oh well, I couldn't worry about that at the time. I was too busy running for my freedom.

Tone and Swift wisely ran into the nearby Cliff Duncan housing projects, and with only two cops about a half block of distance between them, the odds were quickly drifting in their favor to escape. My chances, however, were beginning to look bleak as more attention was turned onto me.

"Stop and put your hands where we can see them!" one cop yelled, as he raced towards me.

Not too familiar with the area, my choices were rather limited. The wrong move on my part may have landed me in the next day's police blotter with a caption that read: Black Man Shot Over Foiled Drug Deal.

I had laughed many a time over the defense having to stay after football practice to run extra laps, but never again. I was exhausted and began to slow down and gasp for air. I quickly turned into a dark corner and raced past a small playground, followed by an abandoned church and a Laundromat. Not thinking twice, I sped past the Laundromat only to soon read a sign that really put the nail in the coffin for me: DEAD END.

With my luck quickly running out, I turned the corner only to hear more sirens, and they were getting louder. The boys in blue must have called in for reinforcement. I was again surrounded, and the same officer that told me to stop made his request for a second time and much louder than before.

"Get down on the ground NOW!"

"Okay…okay!" I responded, instinctively knowing my luck had just run out.

As instructed, I got down on all fours, then laid down and placed my arms behind me so the boys in blue wouldn't find any reason to let off a couple of rounds in my direction. I was quickly cuffed and placed into the back seat of a squad car, wondering how I got myself into that situation.

Not only did I have to endure a weekend in detainment for

my alleged role in a narcotics transaction, but I had to deal with the look of disappointment from my girl Angel. Because I was making my way over to Tone's car during the raid, I was able to state to my lawyer that I was simply going over to greet a couple of long lost acquaintances. No one bought my alibi, but I had nothing on me at the time. More importantly, I had no prior arrests that the defense attorney could get me on.

"You're gonna end up just like your father and brother," Angel angrily said to me. "And didn't you have a game this weekend?"

Damn! I had missed my game. And not just any game…a PLAYOFF game! How would I explain that one to my coaches and teammates?

"Please don't lecture me, not now. Please just take me back to my brother's house."

"See, Prentice, that's what I'm talking about. You've changed. You were just released from being locked away all weekend with them thugs and criminals, and all you can think about is your brother."

"That's right, Angel. Because he's MY brother! And what do you mean I'm gonna end up like Innocent and my father? One lives in a small mansion in Connecticut, and the other in a bad-a** house in one of the best parts of Brooklyn! They own a successful trucking company that I could be working at right now but turned down! Both have loads of money. More money than you and I will ever see PUT TOGETHER! Crazy respect in the streets! What's so bad about that? I'm runnin' around here worrying about how I'm gonna pay for school, bustin' my a** trying to maintain a 'B' average, and for what?"

"You think that's all that matters in this world, Prentice? Money? Respect? A large house? None of that means anything if you're locked up and can't enjoy any of it. Or worse…in a coffin somewhere buried six feet under."

Nonetheless, I was taken back to my brother's house to again explain my absence all weekend. Upon my arrival,

Innocent and Trip were standing at the front door watching my nephew slide down the railing leading to the bottom of the steps.

"I heard through the grapevine you did a quick bid in the joint," Trip chuckled.

"Your girl must be mad as hell, too, the way she just drove off without even saying bye to your sorry a**!" Innocent added.

"The two of y'all have jokes, huh?"

Innocent then proceeded to fill me in on his return from Philly last night, his new sound system for his truck, and his plans for retaliation against the same enemies that firebombed his house. A connect that worked at the DMV gave him the inside tip on who the car was registered to, so revenge would be coming soon. In three days to be exact. One phone call from the connect was all it took to get additional information on the owner of the vehicle. So, not only did Innocent obtain the owner's government name, but also his mailing address and last known telephone number.

An alarm went off on Trip's cell phone.

"Oh snap! I gotta be out, y'all."

"Where you goin' in such a hurry?" I questioned.

Before Trip had a chance to respond, Innocent butted in.

"He's gotta make a drop over on St. James Place at three o'clock p.m. on the third of every month. Go and take the ride with Trip so he can explain it all to you."

"Here we go again. I told you a million times that I'm not tryin' to get down with all of that."

"Oh yeah? Since when? Since an hour ago? You just left out of the joint because you were hanging around a bunch of knuckleheads. And now you're going to stand here and tell me that you can't make a little run for your brother? Your blood? Go and take this ride with Trip. Nothing is going to happen to you."

Seemed like déjà vu. First, it was Tone and Swift, and now, Trip. Talk about walking out of the frying pan and into the fire!

David L.

I prayed he wouldn't get me locked up again.

Trip and I rolled up to 1234 St. James Place with about three minutes to spare. On the ride down, Trip explained the drop, what was being picked up in return, and the individuals involved in the transaction. Out of lockup less than twenty-four hours ago, I was already involved in illegal business again.

"See the lockbox above the mail slot on that building?" Trip asked.

"Yeah, what about it?"

"There should be five thousand in an envelope. Keep the car runnin'. I'll be right back."

Doing as instructed, I reclined my seat back and waited for Trip to return, at the same time, watching his every move. He paused momentarily, walked up one flight of steps, and pulled a key out of his pocket. Then, proceeding as planned, he pulled an envelope out of the lockbox and placed an unidentified bag in its place.

"Five thousand dollars just to do that once a month?" I said to myself. "Maybe I am in the wrong business."

No, I couldn't think like that. I was not my brother...or my father. I was better than that. Trip got me out of my daydreaming daze.

"You better not be in there messin' wit' my CD's or else...," he said, while walking toward the car.

"Or what? Most of them are bootleg anyway! When are you going to step up and spend some money for the real copy? You make way too much money to be so cheap."

"That's okay, young'n. I'm gonna be cheap 'til the day I die! Count on it!"

A loud noise from an undetermined location stopped Trip in

66

mid conversation and startled the hell out of both of us.

BANG! BANG!

The two gunshots were quickly followed by one more gunshot from inside the apartment. Whoever the shooter was, he was wearing a black hooded sweatshirt and what looked to be a handkerchief that covered the majority of his face.

Trip was alert enough to throw the envelope containing the money into the car and motion for me to slide over to the driver's side. He tried to get in through the open window but was unsuccessful as he was only able to slide in halfway. Another loud bang could be heard. Then Trip dropped face first onto the ground and his body hit the pavement. He was now covered with blood and groaning in pain, all while holding the back of his neck.

By now, the shooter had directed his attention to me. However, I had already put Trip's car into drive and floored the pedal. There was nothing I could do to help Trip. Only GOD could spare his life. One more gunshot could be heard as it made contact with the rear window. Once again, I heard the unmistakable sound of police sirens as I placed the envelope into my pocket and ditched the car in a nearby parking lot.

Trip's blood was splattered all over the windows and hood of the car, so it was safe to say I wouldn't have been using his car again. Having learned a lot from my brother and pops throughout the years, I quickly located a towel in the trunk of the car and attempted to wipe my fingerprints from the door handles and steering wheel.

I didn't get a good look at the shooter, but it had to be a set up. What else could it have been? From what Trip told me on the ride down, it was his first drop. So, only a handful of individuals knew about the arrangement. My first course of action was to get into the nearest cab. Destination: Innocent's house.

Word of Trip's untimely demise didn't take long to get back to Innocent. Immediately after the shooting, Trip's assailant

tipped Innocent off about what just went down at the drop off.
Innocent knew minutes before I called to inform him that I was
in a cab and on my way back to his house with the money Trip
slipped me. Rumor of an internal snitch was also used sparingly
as I entered my brother's house.

"Where's Trevor?" Innocent asked no one in particular.
My pops was there, too, and was pacing frantically, which
was somewhat surprising since he was usually so laid back. I
gave them my story over and over again and prepared to make
my exit, as Angel was waiting for me outside. Before I left, I
was grilled by my pops and Innocent at least a dozen more
times regarding what I saw and everything that happened before
Trip got riddled with bullets from his assailant's gun. Growing
more and more impatient, Angel began beeping her car horn.

"What is so important that you couldn't tell me over the
phone?" I questioned.

"Some things are better said face to face," Angel responded.

"So what? You breakin' up with me over what happened
with Tone and Swift? Or is it because I had to spend some time
at my brother's house?"

"See, there you go. Always thinking the worse. It's nothing
like that."

My facial expression and overall demeanor was of
indifference as I waited with anticipation until we got to our
destination. I hadn't even gotten a call from Tone or Swift.
Probably because they knew I wasn't going to let neither one of
them hear the end of their botched caper that landed me in jail
for the weekend.

Angel drove around Kings County Hospital in a circle a few
times before I came to the conclusion that the hospital was our
destination and she was looking for a parking spot. I was
usually much more perceptive; however, Trip's shooting still
had me rattled and unnerved. I dared not tell her what went
down with Trip. She would find out eventually anyway, which
would only get her even angrier with my involvement.

"So are you going to tell me why we're making a stop here? Is someone sick?"

"No, nothing like that. I have a doctor's appointment, that's all."

"That's it? C'mon now. You had me all worried over a doctor's appointment? It's nothing serious, right?"

There was momentary silence as Angel's warm, inviting eyes locked onto mine. She then grabbed my hand and apologized profusely for being so moody over the past several days, promising to show better restraint next time I was called upon to help out a family member. Before responding, her grip on my hand grew even tighter.

"I'm pregnant."

CHAPTER SIX

I t was a day of reflection and remorse. Innocent had not been the same since Trip's death, and he was running around trying to determine who his next lieutenant was going to be. Trip was more than just his right-hand man; he was considered a friend. That was a title not given to many considering what my brother did for a living. I asked him about his longtime ally Trevor, but he conveniently avoided answering my question.

This time, both Innocent and my pops asked me to take the ride down to New Jersey. My pops had been dealing a long time with a gun connect who operated out of a warehouse in Paterson. Later that evening, Innocent's plan was to personally head over to his target's home and let off a few rounds. A subtle reminder of who the real king of New York was. There was just one problem: getting the firepower necessary to make it happen. My brother had not fired a gun in well over three years. He never had to. Someone on his team was always more than ready and willing to do the deed for him.

"So what kind do you want? I got the ARES with a 9 by 19 millimeter cartridge right here. I also got an American 180 with a .22 long rifle cartridge. Then I got the Calico 960 with the parabellum cartridge. Oh yeah, what about right here? I got this Spectre M4 straight outta Italy. Everyone I've sold one to has loved it."

That was Dillinger, the gun connect. He could get any gun ever made on the planet. All you had to do was give him a name of a gun, and if he did not already have it, he could get it for you…and most of the time with no bodies attached to it.

"You got anything I don't need a weightlifting belt to pick up?" Innocent joked. "Those are too bulky for my taste."

"Here, try this one…the Ruger MP9. It's made here in the states, so I can give you a good price for it. You like?"

"Feels good. Not too heavy. How much?"

"It's got a range of up to one hundred meters and lets off up to six hundred rounds per minute."

"How much?"

"It's got a blowback release action and comes with a 32-round box magazine."

"How much!"

"We can talk about the price later. Come sit down and let's get down to why you're really here."

As Innocent walked around the warehouse checking out his many choices of arsenal, my pops had taken the time to school me on the subtle nature of negotiation.

"The first thing you absolutely never want to do is get the first thing offered to you," he said.

"Why?"

"Because the seller's job is to unload their inventory by any means necessary. To get rid of the product that no one else wants."

"Always?"

"Nothing is always, but most of the time. That's why Innocent hasn't dropped any money down yet on the table. It's not because he don't have it. Hell, he can buy this whole warehouse right now if he wanted. It's because I taught him well."

Although my pops and I were never as close as he was to Innocent, I knew he took pride whenever he thought he was teaching me something – illegal or otherwise.

Innocent finally made his selection: the Calico 960 and about ten more assorted handguns for some of his troops. He eyed them up and down with his best poker face and talked Dillinger down one thousand dollars. Not bad for a twenty-minute ride over the George Washington Bridge.

We are all at Innocent's house and within minutes of retaliation. The only difference is this was one ride I definitely would not be taking. I wanted so badly to pick up Innocent's new purchase and hold it in my hand, but feared getting any prints on it. I've held a gun before, but nothing that could do as much death and destruction as what I was looking at. If Angel got word that I went out with my brother for what looked to be a gun fest, she would never forgive me. I still hadn't gotten a call from Tone or Swift. Both were probably too embarrassed about leaving me to fend for myself against the boys in blue.

"Here comes Trevor now with one of his soldiers," my pops said.

Anytime both my pops and Innocent did a drive-by, you knew it was serious. They never went out on jobs together. My pops said that wasn't how you conducted business, which was similar to playing chess. It was too risky in case something was to happen to both of them at the same time.

"You got everything loaded?" my pops asked, looking over at Innocent as he paced outside on the front porch.

Both Crystal and little T.J. were begging him not to go…to send someone else instead. But, that was not my brother's concern that evening. He wanted vindication for the trauma that had inflicted his fortress, and just as importantly, vindication for his right-hand man Trip. The altercation that would unfold was definitely more personal than business. My brother would have it no other way.

"You sure you don't wanna take this ride with us, little brother?" Innocent questioned.

The look on my face gave him his answer. He knew full well that I still hadn't forgiven him one hundred percent for that little side project he had me do with Trip that led to his shooting.

"Leave him alone. He's not built for this. Not yet anyways," my pops added.

Trevor and his partner were busy loading up their ride. Their arsenal paralleled my brother's arsenal in both quantity and force. It did not take a gun expert to tell they meant business that night.

With darkness finally settling and the evening air becoming colder, my brother grew more anxious. He was a victim of the code of the streets and had been privately looking forward to this day since he received that fateful letter threat. I was asked to watch over Crystal and little T.J. until they got back, just in case our "visitors" popped back up for an impromptu visit.

Everyone drove off at approximately seven o'clock. My brother was driving, my pops was in the passenger seat, and following closely behind them was Trevor with someone new that I was never formally introduced to. And me? I was left behind with an upset baby mama and a hyperactive nephew who was keeping himself busy by running over my foot with his toy truck.

Some more of Innocent's crew arrived at 145 Bristol Street to await their intended target: Corey "Big Country" Briggs. He was a burly, three hundred plus individual known throughout his neighborhood for being an enforcer for his big boss – a man simply known as Preemo. He had been reportedly running his drug empire throughout Brooklyn for well over a decade, which was about nine years and six months more than most people survived in this game. Preemo was also allegedly rumored to own stock in over three after-hour clubs, a couple of cab companies, and even a casino somewhere out in Westchester County, New York.

"Call his place and see if he picks up," Crime said to Innocent.

Doing as instructed, the call was made and a young-sounding female voice answered. "He went out to the store and said he would be right back."

The voice belonged to Big Country's daughter, and after about sixty seconds of phone conversation, it was decided upon that the crew would wait for him to return home and try to ex him out without the use of all their accompanying firepower. Similar to Tony Montana, my brother and pops made it a strict rule never to include women and children in their dealings with the opposing enemy – no matter what. If not, Big Country's daughter would've been an easy casualty – all for the sake of revenge.

"He's pulling up to the building now," Innocent said. "The license plate matches up exactly. We got him!"

"Sit tight. We're not gonna get him here. Not outside. Too many witnesses. We'll get him in his apartment," Crime responded. "And we have to be discreet. Everything we do, we do with stealth and cunning. We don't have no time for reckless abandonment of emotions…even if he did firebomb your home and threaten your lady and child. Understand?"

"Understood."

Big Country took his time getting out of his vehicle, which only added to the already elevated intensity level. Innocent had been patiently waiting for this day, and he would not be denied. Unable to reveal their presence for fear of a botched contract, my brother and pops instructed their other two crew members to wait for Big Country up on the seventh floor where he resided.

Preemo's enforcer finally got out of his ride and took the elevator up to his floor. Innocent's people, who were watching his every move, waited for him to pull out his apartment keys to open the door. He had a grocery bag in each hand, and again, he took a moment before entering to look up and down the apartment building's hallway.

"Hurry up before he puts the lock on," one crew member said to the next.

Both rushed over to the door and allowed themselves access to the inside of Big Country's apartment, closing the door behind them.

"WHAT THE...?"

With guns drawn, Big Country was commanded to sit down and await further instruction. On cue, Innocent made his way upstairs and entered the apartment, while my pops waited in the car reading the real estate section of the day's newspaper. Now bound and gagged, Big Country was helpless to whatever Innocent had planned for him.

"Turn the volume up on the television and take the tape off of his mouth. I wanna hear him scream," Innocent said. "Who else is here?"

"My daughter is in the back room with her headphones on. Leave her outta this. She's got nothing to do with any of this."

"You want me to leave her out of this, huh? Kinda like my lady and son had nothing to do with you comin' at me the other night. Mutha******, you almost burned my house down!"

Big Country did not respond, which according to Innocent only gave more insight into his guilt. While both crew members and Innocent had their firepower aimed at him, one of Trevor's partners went to the back room to check on his daughter. As expected, she was watching cartoons with her headphones on – totally oblivious to what was transpiring in the very next room. Trevor, who had just made his way into the apartment, motioned to Innocent that he was going back down to the lobby to make sure no unexpected visitors arrived. Weapons still drawn, a crew member recommended to Innocent to go into the kitchen to take Big Country out of his misery with a large knife instead to avoid all of the unnecessary noise from the automatic gun he was wielding in his hand.

"You won't kill me, Innocent. If you do, Preemo will have your a** for breakfast!" Big Country said.

"Oh really? Before we part ways, there was another person with you when you came to my house and tried to take out my family. Who is he? What's his name?" Innocent questioned.

"I'll take that to my grave before I rat anyone out. You can believe that! If you're gonna do anything, then do it! I'm a soldier!"

So you'd rather die than give me a name? You're really that loyal to someone that probably wouldn't do the same for you?"

"You're gonna kill me anyway. And if I did give you a name, then I'm as good as dead by sundown. Best believe that. My boss would have me floating in the river or buried somewhere in a matter of no time. So, go 'head and do what you gotta do. At least no one will accuse me of going out like a b***h!"

"It's your funeral!"

"Not just my funeral! Yours, too! Before you take me out of my misery, I will tell you this…keep your enemies close and your friends closer!"

"Whatever. He's not gonna talk. Tell GOD I said I'll see him when I get there!"

Without hesitation, Innocent looked Big Country directly in his eyes and told him to say a prayer before he met his maker. He then proceeded to slit his throat, watching in glee as the blood poured down his lifeless corpse, with some of it getting on my brother's new three-hundred-dollar alligator shoes.

"Let's get the hell out of here!" Innocent said, looking down at his stained gators.

There was no answer from the back room. Once again, the front door was forced open. This time, however, four armed officers appeared, all with body armor and one large police dog ready to pounce on the first thing that moved. With their weapons drawn on my brother, it gave Trevor's partners in the back room ample time to make their way down the fire escape.

Like I said before, my brother's nickname came from over twenty charges in which he was let off the hook over some type of formality. With a dead body bound and gagged in a chair, fingerprints on the murder weapon that laid dormant just a few feet away, and his victim's blood on his shoes, I was curious to know how he would get out of that one.

I was separated from my brother by about three inches of glass. We were holding phones to our ears to hear the other one talk. He was wearing the state-issued orange jumpsuit that was required by all prisoners at Elmira Correctional Facility, and every move he made got the attention of the two guards that were positioned strategically in the corners of the visitor's room area. For a man who had just been sentenced to life without the possibility of parole, he was rather laid back and relaxed.

"I need you to hold me down out there, kid. Don't let me go out like this."

"You know I can't get down with you. I got school. I've already ruined my chances at a real football scholarship messin' around with you and Pops. Did you know my team won their playoff game without me?"

"Stop talking nonsense. The family needs you more than ever. Pops isn't gonna be able to run the trucking company by himself. He's got workers, but it's not the same."

"Tammy and her loser boyfriend can help out. Hell, he needs a job more than anybody I know!"

"You're talking scared right now because of what happened

to me. I understand. I know a natural when I see one. You were born for this."

"See, that's where you're wrong, big bro. I'm NOT built for this. I can barely see you like this!"

"Like what? I'm here 'cause I got sloppy. I let my emotions take over. No way should I have put myself in that type of situation. That's what I got soldiers ready to die for me for."

"What about Pops? He was the man before you, so why can't he be the man now once again?"

There was silence followed by some hand tapping by my brother and then a few more seconds of silence.

"Pops is dying. He's got cancer. I just found out about a month ago."

"And you didn't tell me?"

"Lower your voice. You ain't that grown just 'cause I'm stuck up in here."

"Does Tammy know?" I asked.

"Nobody knows except you, me, and the doctor that told him."

"Yo, Innocent, whatever happened to all those guns you purchased out in Jersey?"

"Watch what you say up in here. This whole place is probably bugged. They're stashed somewhere safe from anyone getting to them. Why?"

"No reason. Hey, what about Trevor? Besides Trip, wouldn't he have been next in line to take over the operation? Keep money on the table?"

Again, there was more silence followed by what appeared to be deep thought, which was something my brother always did when he wanted to make sure he got his point across without saying the wrong thing.

"F**k that snake-in-the-grass n***a! I don't trust his a** one bit. For all I know, Trevor's the reason why I'm here now."

When one of the guards walked over to Innocent, he quickly lowered his voice.

I always sensed a disconnect between Trevor and my brother, and the facts spoke for itself. Trevor had not been by once yet to see him after the verdict was handed down, and he had always conveniently been MIA whenever there was a shakedown. And how come his corrupt cop ally, Lincoln, didn't warn Innocent of the undercover sting on Big Country's apartment? I half expected Innocent to finally come down from off of his high horse and be humbled by his situation, but no – not yet anyway. From the way he talked, you would think he was doing the same weekend stint I finished doing a few weeks previously.

He motioned me closer to the glass, as if pulling my chair up would make a difference.

"I won't get too much into it 'cause I don't trust these phones," he began. "I need you to run my operation – both the trucking company and what I do out in the street. Make me proud. I have enough money stashed away and firepower to start a borough war if need be. Recruit some soldiers that you trust and avenge my prison sentence. Get the ones that did this to me. Can I count on you, lil' brother? Look me in my eyes and tell me you will bring my enemies to justice."

There was more silence and hesitation, but that time on my part. Watching your own flesh and blood – your hero growing up – plead for you to help them carryout their revenge on their foes would do that to you.

"Yeah, man, I'll do it," I finally said out of frustration.

"Good. Then begin by talking to Pops. He'll walk you through everything."

A tap on Innocent's shoulder was the signal that his time was up. A woman C.O. motioned for him to look up at the clock on the wall, signaling the end of our visit.

"Yo, Innocent, I forgot to tell you. I'm goin' to be a daddy."

Too late. He had already placed the receiver down and was being escorted back to his cell, leaving me with even more on my plate that I was not quite ready to handle.

CHAPTER SEVEN

As long as I had breath in my body and the will to carry on my brother's movement, Innocent's legacy would remain a memory of pride and respect in the streets of Brooklyn and beyond. At least that's what I kept telling myself.

I was no longer paying rent on an apartment I barely stayed at, and I had decided to move in with Crystal and little T.J. until I eventually moved in with Angel and my unborn baby. I wanted to pop the question to Angel, but I didn't want her to think it was only because of the news that she was pregnant.

As promised, my father schooled me about the family business, and whenever my brother got phone privileges, he would fill me in on whatever my pops forgot to mention. Speaking of Crime, I started to see signs of his failing health. He had been taking multiple trips to the doctor's office; he was rapidly losing weight, and he didn't have much energy during the day. He finally got the nerve to tell me the news about having cancer. He had been so preoccupied with being an emotionless robot for all of his years that it touched me to finally see the warm, human element that made up my father.

Although Angel had promised to be more understanding,

her angry moods had elevated and her attitude had worsened. Ever since I had moved into my brother's house, she hadn't been by one time to see me, and had made no attempt to spend any quality time with me. Instead, she had started a new life of hanging out with her own circle of friends and going out to random clubs, which is something she rarely done before.

Right on schedule, Crime rang the bell, and after letting himself in, I motioned him into the living room.

"Did you make those phone calls I told you to make?" he asked. "Since your brother's detainment, there are a lot of individuals out here in the street tryin' to take over at his expense. We need to speed things up."

"Yes, I've called every one of them, but I'm not being taken seriously. Even your boy Trevor hasn't returned any of my phone calls. And that was like three hours ago!"

"Well, forget about him. He probably won't be calling you anytime soon if my suspicions about him are correct. You need to make an example. It only takes one person, but it may have to be a person of influence to work effectively. Trevor is mad because he wasn't the chosen one, but he's gonna have to get over it and move on."

"Easier said than done."

"That's his problem. What 'bout the drop on Franklin Avenue? That has to be made exactly on time. If you got no one to do it for you, do it yourself. Just make sure it gets done. Unless you're tryin' to start a war!"

"That's this weekend, right?"

"Correct. Nine p.m. sharp. Saturday. Do you have anyone that's reliable and you can trust?"

"No. No, I don't. Wait a minute. Yes, I think I do. I just have to get on the phone and call them."

"Well, hurry up and make that call. Time is money!"

Before making my departure, my pops hugged me and placed an envelope in my hand, then put on his coat and got ready to make his departure.

"Aren't you even going to count it?" he said to me.

"For what? You're the last person I have to worry about. Your word is your bond, right? Isn't that what you've been preaching to me since I could remember?"

I don't give a damn what I've taught you, boy! ALWAYS count your money when someone hands it to you. TRUST NO ONE! The ones you trust today will be the same ones that stab you in the back tomorrow. Got it?"

Immediately checking the contents, I noticed it contained thirty thousand dollars in fifty-dollar bills. Ten thousand dollars more than what I expected.

"What's the extra ten thousand for?" I questioned.

"Like everything else in life, respect is gonna cost you…at first anyway. Spread that around and people will look to you for direction and salvation from their own money woes. Plus, you're gonna need some startup money if we're gonna properly prepare you for taking over Innocent's spot."

I called my connect and confirmed the drop for Saturday night. Right afterwards, I made two more phone calls and began setting up my potential list of soldiers, beginning with my two old hangout partners: Swift and Tone.

At my request, Tammy showed up to Innocent's house along with Swift and Tone, who arrived ten minutes late and were immediately scolded by my sister before I had a chance to make any comments about their tardiness. Although I was the official face of the family empire, my brother and father still kept things in check to a certain degree, and my sister still played a good background role. Innocent and my pop's influence transcended the fact that one resided in Connecticut and the other was in jail for the rest of his life.

Crime had stressed for me to create a strong presence from the very beginning and not take any nonsense from anyone – friend and foe alike. Unfortunately, for me, that was way easier said than done. Even with the lure of offering more money per job, Swift and Tone had been doing work for years and may not have wanted to take orders from the "new guy on the block". I went over the drop with everyone again for clarity and to ensure there were no mistakes.

"Swift, I need you to stay put in the car and keep the engine running. If Tone is in the apartment longer than five minutes, go in strapped and be ready to let off some strays. FIVE MINUTES! Give our connects the envelope and double check the supply. Hell, triple check it if you have to! If they start talking too much, they're stalling. Politely ask them to shut the f**k up and count everything all over again! Tammy and I are going to be parked about half a block behind you and will be watching everything from a distance. According to the rules of the contract, Tone is not allowed to walk in strapped, so you have to have his back, Swift. You understand?"

Both Tone and Swift nodded their heads in agreement while taking notes on their PalmPilots. I also let it be known that I had not forgotten about the last botched caper that landed me in the joint for a weekend stay.

"This is your test. After that last escapade y'all put me through, there's a lot to prove here. Don't let me down. There stands to be a lot of money made if everything goes correctly."

"Let you down? I've been in this game since grade school! Now, all of a sudden, you're Al Capone? I remember when you had a paper route!" Tone blurted out.

I nodded my head in feigned agreement and motioned Tammy over to whisper something in her ear. Preferring at least for the immediate moment to ignore Tone's comments, I pulled out a storage box full of firepower and instructed Swift on how to use a Calico automatic. His eyes grew wide with anticipation, and he took great pride in the handling of the weapon as I showed him how to load it. Although little T.J. had seen many a gun in his young life, I redirected him back to his bedroom and to the safety of his video game collection. I refused to further corrupt my young nephew, preferring instead to try and salvage whatever little innocence was left in his body.

"Alright, it's that time. Let's go handle our business," I said. "We have to be there by exactly nine o'clock on the dot, so let's get movin'."

Everyone grabbed their jackets and began heading for the front door, but before we left, some unfinished business needed to be taken care of. On my head nod to Tammy, one of Innocent's longtime enforcers, who went by the name Drac, entered the room. He had been in the kitchen the entire time playing his position and waiting for his time to do what he did best. He had a bat in his hand and a smirk on his face. Probably from the enjoyment that would come from what he was about to do next. With one very well directed blow to Tone's kneecap, Tone crouched over in the corner of the room, screaming in pain. Drac then returned to the kitchen, but not before I looked down at Tone in order for him to acknowledge that it was I who had this done to him. My message was straight with no chaser: Don't f**k with a made man! If my brother and Pop's plan was as correct as I thought it would be, I wouldn't have any more problems from Tone getting out of line ever again.

"Tammy, can you bandage him up please? He's gonna need to be able to use that leg to do his job at the drop off."

It was my first official operation in which I was in charge of everything. I was slightly nervous, but I dared not show it in front of the crew. If anyone were to even get the wiser, my rep would suffer irreparable damage.

We got to our location right on time, while each of us maintained contact with one another through the phones we received from my pop's cell phone connect out in the Bronx.

"That was good work back there at the house, lil' bro. You can't tolerate any dissension from your team. From NOBODY! I mean, sometimes like Pops says, you have to make an example out of someone. Your boy Tone just happened to be that someone," Tammy said to me, while texting her loser boyfriend about her current whereabouts.

Although she had never personally gotten her hands dirty in the family business, she knew the ins and outs of what to do and not do. Truth be told, she probably could have jumped right in and been a key figure in the business. However, my pops swore she would never be directly involved. He wanted her to remain pure and innocent to the dangers of the drug world. Yeah, right! She had seen and heard more than I ever imagined, and she had been anything but pure and innocent since I could remember.

Speaking of setting examples, Tone could be seen limping into the apartment as directed. Swift was in the car with the engine running in case they had to make a quick getaway.

"Tammy, has it been five minutes yet?" I asked.

"Four minutes and counting. Relax for once. I'm keeping count."

Before I got a chance to remind Swift about the plan, I saw him get out of the car and walk up the steps to the apartment. I was his backup until I gathered additional troops, so I got out and instructed Tammy to call Pops if we weren't out in exactly five minutes.

I double checked the apartment number as I walked by and let myself in with my hand on my trigger in case any nonsense came my way. Unaware of whom I would be encountering, my jaw dropped when two beautiful females emerged from what looked to be the kitchen. The apartment smelled like someone spent all day frying up chicken. They were holding plates of food and drink on a dinner tray and wearing uncharacteristically seductive clothing. Across the other side of the room, another well-endowed and beautiful female had her gun pointed in the direction of both Tone and Swift.

"Y'all must be crazy sticking us up. You know this operation is already in the books, right? That means any foul business and y'all will be dead before the morning. I can guarantee that!" I warned.

"What makes you think we plan on sticking y'all up? Because we have guns drawn?" the one holding the gun said back to me. "We just wanted your attention! Matter of fact, as a sign of goodwill, we made all of you some dinner. That's our way of showing your brother and father that we wanna switch over to a winning team."

"And you're trying to get my attention by drawing your guns on me and my men?"

"It worked, didn't it?" another one of the women said.

I carefully thought about her question for a moment and smirked. They were all drop-dead beautiful, smart, and dangerous. A winning combination if I had ever seen one.

"Yeah, I guess it did. Put your guns down and let's talk for a moment."

I immediately alerted Tammy that everything was okay, but only after their weapons were lowered. Tammy decided to wait in the car while the rest of us exchanged pleasantries. The rest of the evening seemed more like an interview than a business transaction. All three women were well versed in the martial arts, fluent in both Espanol and English, and knew more about guns than Tone, Swift, and I put together. Their names? On the independent circuit, they went by the Chica Clique, three crazy Hispanic b*****s that were down for whatever and prided themselves on being free agents and not having to answer to any boss.

Normally not one to mix business with pleasure, I made an exception and indulged in some of their cooking. Tone was still visibly shaken up from being held at gunpoint, and Swift was trying his best to show that he wasn't outsmarted by a bunch of crafty females.

"Y'all girls do interstate runs?" I questioned.

Jackie, who appeared to be the leader of the trio, responded, "We do interstate runs, out-of-the-country runs…hell, I'll do a run to the mayor's house if it pays enough!"

"Do any of you have any priors? Meaning when you're pulled over by the boys in blue."

"None of us has ever done any time…EVER! No arrests. No fingerprints. Hell, I don't think I even have any points on my driver's license!" Jackie said.

"So you know my brother well?"

"I know enough between him and Crime that if you're taking over, I'm either gonna get down or lay down! Personally, I'd rather get down, if you know what I mean."

"Yeah, I think I do. Thank you, ladies. We'll definitely be in touch."

Phone numbers were exchanged and a few more pieces of the best fried chicken this side of Brooklyn was grabbed as we made our departure. As we drove off, I informed Tammy that I thought I had just found the missing pieces to my newly-formed empire. Now it was time to get back at the ones that sent Innocent away for the rest of his life.

Along with his daily battle with cancer, my pops had gotten a tip from one of his police informants that there was a warrant out for his arrest, as well as a bounty from some rival drug lords that had been trying to make a name for themselves. One hundred thousand dollars to be exact. More than likely, the bounty was from the same individuals that put my brother away. Now mainly delegated to hiding out in his Connecticut home, my pops was still pulling strings like a true puppet master from afar.

My next mission was one that was never truly completed by Innocent. To work out an agreement over territory with two aspiring kings of New York: Lord and Wise. I arrived in the Fort Greene section of Brooklyn, along with Tone, Swift, and Drac, and the neighborhood was populated with crack fiends and pushers of all ages. From the teenage girl who appeared to be hooking out of the front seat of a mini-van to the middle-aged man who was driving it. This was no average contract negotiation, and we needed all the muscle that I could muster. My new recruits, the Chica Clique, were much more finesse than force, and I had much more creative aspirations for them other than local scores like that one. So, I instructed them to handle another side project for the time being.

"So you're the new go-to man, huh? It's very unfortunate how things went down with your brother. I was privately pulling for him to skate through myself. I wouldn't wish that on my worst enemy," Lord said.

One of the first lessons taught to me by my father was silence speaks volumes, so I nodded my head to acknowledge Lord's remarks.

He and Wise had visible bulges around their waist, alerting me to the fact that both were probably strapped and more than willing to pull out if necessary.

"So how much phone time has Innocent been getting? I know he's still runnin' things from inside the joint," Lord added.

"He's gotta be. Innocent is no fool. You think he's gonna let little brother with the book bag on his back run everything?"

It was finally all starting to make sense. The two of them were feeling me out, looking for a weak spot in my armor. But, unbeknownst to either of them, that was not going to happen. Not on my watch anyway.

"I run the family business now. Me. Nobody else. So when

do we come to an agreement about what was discussed with my brother before he got put away?"

We were all motioned into what looked to be an abandoned building and a very deserted apartment studio. No wonder Lord had so much money. He never spent any of it! He was notorious for being frugal and could often be seen driving around in a hooptie and wearing a played-out sweat suit and rundown sneakers. As expected, we were offered drinks as a sign of peace; however, I respectfully declined, just like I was instructed to do by my brother.

"So let's get down to business," Lord said.

"I've got other things going on right now," I declared. "Things that take priority over trying to outmuscle every nickel-and-dime pusher out here tryin' to get their pockets in order."

"So what are you tryin' to say? You don't want to negotiate?"

"Not at all. If that was the case, I could've called you instead of making the trip all the way up here and wasting both of our time. To tell you the truth, you can have all the way to Utica Avenue. You won't get any resistance from us," I solemnly promised.

"That was easy! What's the catch?" Wise questioned.

Swift and Tone had a look of bewilderment on their faces. Mainly because they knew Innocent and Crime would have something to say when the word got back to them about the change in plans.

"No catch. I am hereby relinquishing my entire stake in Utica Avenue. But, I need something from you. Something I think only you can assist me with. What do you say?"

Lord pulled out a cigar, bit the head off, and lit it. Then he proceeded to take a pull which emanated a smoke ring in my direction. Wise, his lieutenant, was fidgeting in his chair, which was beginning to make me nervous. Since I was the only one armed at the time, partly because I didn't one hundred percent trust Tone after what I had done to him, we were outgunned.

"So don't keep me in suspense. What do you need from me?" Lord asked.

I took a moment to gather my thoughts and choose my words wisely, just like Innocent would have done in a similar situation.

"I want information on how I can catch up to the individual known as Preemo. I need to know where he hangs out and who he hangs out with. Everything you know about the man. Can you do that?"

Lord and Wise chuckled at my request. Then it was Lord's turn to take a moment to gather his thoughts and take another pull from his cigar.

"You want Preemo, huh? Trust me, once word gets out that you're looking for him, he will make it a point to find *you.* That's for certain!"

"I was counting on that."

Lord and Wise chuckled again at the nerve of my request. Nevertheless, Lord promised to give me what I needed within twenty four hours, but only as long as I kept my word about keeping my troops away from his newly-acquired territory.

I was officially one step closer to vindication. It was about to be on!

I finally made it to my destination, which was LaGuardia Airport. Upon being dropped off by Drac for a last-minute run to the ATL to handle some business that none of my pop's truckers could handle, Swift and I barely got past airport security because of all the miscellaneous crap Swift was trying to board the plane with: mouthwash, soda, shower gel, deodorant. The list went on and on.

"What did you bring all that stuff for anyway, Swift? We're

only gonna be down there for the weekend."

"I'm trying to hit the club when we get down there. I don't know about you, but I have to be on point. I have to let those ATL chicks know a real Brooklyn playa is in the building!"

The run to Atlanta was a no-brainer and my first official major out-of-state business contract. If everything went according to plan, the family would be one hundred thousand dollars richer by Monday morning. There was only one downside to everything: I had never been on a plane before, and just the mere sight of the inside of the plane had me ready to regurgitate all over the place.

"Are you gonna make it? You look bad," Swift said, stating the obvious.

"I need some of those sleeping pills my sister hooked me up with. Only problem is I think they were checked in with the rest of our bags."

One overly enthusiastic stewardess offered me a cocktail to help relieve my nerves. It was not until after my third drink that I began to relax. Eventually, the plane landed safely, and I narrowly avoided embarrassing myself with my air sickness.

"See, you made it," Swift joked.

"I didn't make s**t! I still have to go back on that damn thing for the ride back."

With only two days to take care of business, we promised one another that we were going to take in some sights and dabble in the club scene while down there. Neither of us had travelled extensively in our lifetimes, and knowing the mortality rate for us being in the business we were in, we swore to live life to its fullest.

"Why didn't your pops just have the money wired to New York?" Swift asked.

"'Cause I think he's testing me. He knows about my fear of flying. He also knows I've never really been anywhere in my life. If we're going to continue to grow, I'm going to have to get used to the fact that I will be doing a lot of traveling, and he's very big on first-time encounters. He likes to see the people he is either giving money to or receiving money from. He says it's the only way he can look them in the eyes and see what they're truly about."

Everything went according to plan, and upon our destination to Northlake Mall where we previously designated to meet our business associates, they were already awaiting our arrival. Like true businessmen, a briefcase was handed to me and they both looked on as I counted the currency which added up down to the last bill. Their names? It didn't matter, because according to my pops, they planned on selling their car dealership business and moving down to Miami for an early retirement. They were a couple of suit and tie wearing, BMW driving, republican White boys that exuded professionalism and courtesy.

"With that over with, let's go hit a club. One of my boys tells me there's this live joint somewhere on Jimmy Carter Boulevard," Swift said.

"You go ahead and enjoy yourself," I replied. "But, first, drop me off at a car rental joint. I'm driving my Black a** back to New York!"

CHAPTER EIGHT

To say my life had picked up in the next several weeks would be an understatement of major proportions. Angel was in the final week of her first trimester, and I was busy planning a surprise party for her in which I was going to propose. I was watching my pop's health take a turn for the worse as he battled cancer, and my street legend credibility was steadily growing in leaps and bounds. I had not heard from Trevor in weeks, and his cell phone appeared to be deactivated. I privately felt Swift had the potential to be my future lieutenant. However, he sometimes allowed his emotions to override his logical intuition. Tone was borderline incompetent at times and would sometimes get taken advantage of by up and comers. One day, that fool made an out-of-state run to Delaware and got pulled over for getting busted talking on his cell phone. To top it off, when the policeman walked over to the car, he had a bag of money in the passenger seat!

"Why won't you let me pack a gun?" Tone asked.

"'Cause you don't always make the best decisions," I responded. "Like yesterday for example. How is anyone gonna take you seriously when you let a little twelve-year-old beat you

David L.

out of five hundred dollars? I told you over and over again –
count the entire stack of money. Not just whatever is on top.
The whole thing!"
   I was referring to a contract that took place the day before
over in the Brownsville section of Brooklyn with a new crew of
up and comers who had a reputation of taking no s**t from
anybody. They shot first, asked questions later, and took pride in
getting over on your friendly neighborhood drug dealer. The
catch? None of them were older than sixteen! Just the added
element I needed for my eventual takeover. Lord and Wise
could have Utica Avenue. I had bigger thoughts like taking over
all five boroughs one day. What a change from the mild-
mannered individual who was once studying for his Bachelor's
Degree and contemplated playing professional football.
   My thoughts were interrupted by a text from my pops
alerting me that Lincoln, the crooked cop, was headed over to
the diner where I was presently eating with Swift and Tone.
   "What happened to the original spot?" Tone questioned.
   "The spot on St. James was raided a couple of nights ago.
Everything's starting to get hot, so he wants to collect his
money himself and meet up with us at the diner. Everything
remains the same. Just a new location."
   "What has he done for him to be getting our hard-earned
money anyways?"
   "Nothing yet, but I don't want to rock the boat. My pops
says pay the man, so we pay the man. Understood? That must
be him right there getting out of his car," I said, taking a bite out
of my burger. "He fits the description. He even looks and walks
like a dirty cop."
   Sure enough, Lincoln walked over to where we were all
sitting and introduced himself. He was there for his five
thousand dollar monthly fee, which I reluctantly handed over in
an unmarked envelope. He counted the money three times
before placing it into his back pocket – very discreetly of
course.

96

"I hate to do this to you, but I'm gonna have to increase my price," he said.

He was talking to us, but avoided any prolonged eye contact as he kept himself busy looking out the diner window.

"I never quite understood how Innocent wasn't notified that there was a sting operation on the exact same night he paid a visit to Big Country," I responded.

"I had no knowledge of that operation," Lincoln replied. "There was nothing I could do about that, but I've warned your brother before about being in the streets. He was supposed to have been making his moves from a phone…or behind a desk like a true executive."

"How much more money are you charging me?"

"I'll call you. I have your number."

Lincoln then proceeded to order a turkey sandwich and a coffee, and motioned to the waitress to put it on my tab. Everyone at the table looked at me to see my response, but I remained level-headed so as to not give away my true emotions. I could see that Lincoln was going to have to be another unfortunate casualty added to my growing list of names to be terminated.

Angel had agreed to meet me back at the house to discuss our future together. Luckily, she was pressed for time and wouldn't be hanging around long. Besides, I was expected to meet up with my pops somewhere out in Yonkers along with my newly-formed team: Swift, Tone, Drac, and Jackie, who was also representing for her other two partners. Neither could be present because they were working the evening shift at Sonny's, a popular strip club located in Downtown Brooklyn.

"What did you do to your hair?" I asked.

"You like? I just got my hair done. I'm going out with some of my girls tonight," Angel responded.

Not the jealous type by any means, I nodded my head approvingly. I did mention her growing need to hang out at the clubs with her many girlfriends and neglect of me. Even worse, she was neglecting our unborn child by partying night after night.

"I meant what I said before, Prentice," Angel warned. "If you continue to live this life, you and I aren't going to work. I lost an uncle to drugs, and I have another one doing ten years for selling. For all I know, maybe either your pops or Innocent sold the drugs to them. Do you hear what I'm sayin'?"

"I hear you."

"You hear me, but are you listening? I'm serious, Prentice. You and I are having this child together! I don't want to be just another single mother out here whose baby daddy is locked up somewhere or worse dead because he was too blind to see what was happening before it was too late."

"And I'm serious. This life isn't me. It's just temporary. Matter of fact, I plan on telling my pops in the next few days that I can no longer do this. It's just that he doesn't have much time left, that's all." I knew that was a low blow, using my father's illness to my advantage, but I had to think quickly.

The rest of the crew arrived just as Angel pulled out of the driveway. The agenda: pay a visit to the Dynasty Lounge later that evening. About an hour previously, I had finally gotten my very delayed phone call from Lord, who earlier promised to give me information on where I could catch up to the man simply known as Preemo. I didn't expect too much to happen, but if nothing else, I needed to establish a presence. Let him know his days were numbered – but tactfully of course. My sister Tammy also showed up to the house to lend her two cents.

"He usually gets to the Dynasty Lounge around eleven," I said. "We'll confront him there. I will anyways. Drac, I need you positioned directly across from him. You, Tone, and Swift.

Don't do anything. Don't even make eye contact with him."

"What about me?" Jackie questioned.

"You got the most important part. Flirt with him, but don't be too obvious. He's gonna be around his crew members most likely, so try to get him to buy you some drinks or something. Soften him up. Can you handle that?"

"I strip at a gentlemen's club three times a week! I got married men wanting to leave their wives and buy me more drinks than I could ever handle in five lifetimes! Do you really want to ask me that question again?"

"I'm comin', too," Tammy said.

"You can come, but not inside the club. I got something I need you to do for me after we all walk into the lounge. I need you to do it exactly as planned."

"What is it?"

"Be patient. I'll fill you in when the time is right."

Everyone was instructed to go home and get some rest for later that night. Things were going to begin heating up quickly!

The Dynasty Lounge. A place supposedly known for its adult and classy atmosphere filled with power players and larger-than-life individuals. That night, there was also a lot of visibly underage females congregating around outside. There was a line leading inside the establishment, but one of the first things I had learned since taking over the family business was that money talks. I handed the guy at the door a fifty spot, and we all walked in to the dismay of everyone outside still battling the cold air.

"How are you going to be able to tell which one is Preemo?" Swift questioned. "None of us has ever seen him before."

David L.

"Easy. He's got his name tatted on his hand. He is also a drinker. So, Jackie, I need you to work your magic at the bar. See if you can locate him. The rest of us will be at a table in the back corner."

Jackie did as instructed. Again, money did all the talking for me as I persuaded a couple trying to get their romance on to give up their table with another fifty spot. Life was good when you had money to spread around.

I was signaled by Jackie with a text alerting me to Preemo's presence. As expected, he was seated at the bar surrounded by two of his goons. I could see Jackie from the corner of my eye prancing around the bar, looking very alluring and available...a perfect combination. There was jazz music playing in the background, while a spoken word poet recited his most recent poem. He was a classic hippie wannabe adorned in sandals, bell-bottom jeans, and a tight plaid shirt.

The four of us went over the plan once more and positioned ourselves closer to the bar to watch Preemo's every move. He was not quite what I expected in a self-proclaimed "kingpin". He was dressed down and appeared very average looking. He was sipping on some type of girly drink, complete with an umbrella and orange wedge on the side of the cup. Even his mannerisms were very suspect. It was not until I saw the "Preemo" tattoo on his hand that I knew for sure it was him.

I ordered some drinks for everyone and built up my courage for the walk over to the bar. Before doing so, Jackie was whispering something in his ear as she placed what looked to be her phone number on a business card into his front pocket. Then she proceeded to walk away. I motioned to the bartender to get him a "real" drink: straight Hennessey with no ice.

"Enjoy your drink, Preemo. It's on me," I said.

"Who are you and how do you know me?"

"Let's just say your boy Big Country won't be the only one taking a dirt nap. Innocent lives through me now, so watch ya back!"

One of Preemo's goons began rising from his barstool, only to be motioned by Preemo to sit back down. Even with the lights dimmed, I could see the scowl on Preemo's face. He was playing right into my hand. It was pure emotion over logic. Once you get your enemy to react without thought, half the battle has already been won.

"So you're takin' over for Innocent now? You really think you're ready? You're in the big leagues now, son. Watch your back AND everyone else in your family! I hereby pronounce you marked for death."

Preemo paid for his and his crew's drinks and promptly removed himself, with his goons following closely behind. His purchased Hennessey remained untouched in his absence. I, on the other hand, now had my turn to smirk, because I knew I had gotten into his head just like Pops and Innocent taught me to do.

"You and me will be seeing each other again real soon," I announced, as Preemo and company continued their walk towards the exit door.

My eyes followed Preemo's every step as he unlocked his ride with his remote access alarm, only to notice that all four of his tires were now flattened. It was another reminder of what it meant to mess with someone "connected". I watched in glee as he searched his vehicle thoroughly for any unfamiliar devices. A note on his windshield simply read: TAG! YOU'RE IT!

It was March 31st, Angel's birthday, and all of her closest friends and family members were at her apartment to surprise her when she walked in. Unfortunately, it was me who was the only one surprised as she unlocked the door and entered with a male individual right behind her. He was quickly sized up by myself and introduced to everyone by Angel as simply a

---

David L.

"friend". The birthday festivities continued as planned, but not before I had a chance to do some investigating.

"So how come you never mentioned him to me before?" I asked Angel.

"I did mention Dayvon to you before. You just don't listen when I talk to you. He's an old friend from high school who just moved back home. He was in the Navy for a couple of years and recently returned."

"Yeah, whatever. So why is he here? In your apartment?"

"'Cause we were gonna hang out for my birthday...he, I, and a bunch of my girls. I didn't know you were going to throw me a party."

"Well it looks like you got busted! What real man hangs out at a club with a bunch of females? And now I have to face all your people up in here now. People asking me questions I don't have answers to."

Like I've said on many of an occasion, karma is a b***h! Not too long ago on my birthday, my old ex Nicole was sweating me and trying to get with me. Now here I am at my lady's party and I'm dealing with déjà vu.

The remainder of the evening was relatively uneventful, as I was seated on the couch between one of Angel's aunts, who was looking for any conceivable reason to grope me, and one of her perverted old uncles. Angel once confided in me that this son of a b***h used to repeatedly fondle her breasts and rear end when she was a kid. It was a story she had never told anyone else. If I didn't swear to secrecy, I would have slapped the s**t out of him at that exact moment!

"So you're a friend of Angel's, huh?" I said to her male "friend" from high school.

"Yeah, we go way back. We went out for like two or three weeks, but nothing serious or anything like that."

"Look how beautiful she is standing over there. She isn't even showing yet."

"Yeah, that's right. Congratulations! She told me earlier this

102

afternoon."

"Y'all must be close, because there are family members she hasn't even told yet about the baby on the way. You sure y'all only went out for a couple of weeks back in the day?"

Our conversation with one another was of a classic male "pissing on a tree for territory rights" ritual. Our eyes made contact from the time he entered her apartment, so he knew instinctively that I was someone significant. I knew in my gut that he wanted to hit it, and he knew that I knew he wanted to hit it. And Angel was not stupid, so she knew that I knew he wanted to hit it. However, one thing was for sure...if I ever found out that he did hit it, I was going to kill him.

I was so mad by the end of the party that I never did accomplish my sole purpose of the party, which was the proposal.

South Jersey right off the turnpike was my next destination. The time was exactly eleven-thirty at night, and I had to meet up with some of my pop's connects at a Days Inn Hotel to collect seventy-five thousand dollars for a job he did well over a month ago. That was a lot of money to wait on, so my assumption was this was a job that Crime had already finalized without any problems in the past. Along with myself, I had both Tone and Swift, and of course my equalizer Drac for my muscle, whose primary job was to stand speechless and look intimidating. Even in New Jersey, my father's name held plenty of weight in the streets.

"Word on the street is Crime is really stressing that hundred thousand bounty on his head," one of my pop's connects said to me.

"He's not too concerned about that," I responded.

"Sure about that? I've heard of a few people that wouldn't mind collecting on that bounty money."

There were three of them total, and they were doing their best to appear just as intimidating. However, I could see through their façade of insecurity. The way one of them held the money clutched to his side. Another avoided eye contact at all costs. The third one was sweating and it was about thirty degrees outside!

"I'm not worried about any bounty," I responded with confidence. "Neither is Crime. I'm here because I'm the new face of the family. And the n***a who put the bounty out – well, let's just say I got him on my radar!"

The overall cash transaction went as smoothly as expected, albeit kind of time-consuming. There was too much talk of bounty money and talk of Crime's supposed retirement. It was almost as if those three connects were looking forward to my father's demise, and it wasn't just my imagination either. Both Tone and Swift commented on their preoccupation with how much of a bounty was on my father's head.

Out of the hotel with a suitcase full of my pop's money, I began to wonder how they knew of the bounty in the first place. It wasn't like my pops to say anything to them about it. He didn't talk about his personal business like that to anyone, especially a bunch of low-level clowns whose names were never even given to me to add to my collection of names of top priority contacts. I was only a few feet away from Innocent's Range Rover that I'd been driving since his incarceration, when I stopped suddenly in my tracks.

"What's the matter?" Tone questioned.

"Yeah, what's up? Let me in the truck. It's cold as hell out here!" Swift added.

"Something ain't right," I responded.

Nonetheless, the numbness in my fingers from the cold air reminded me of just how cold it was out there. The headlights from the Range Rover alerted me to the fact that we had unexpected company.

"I knew it! It's a f*****g setup!"

Headlights from another vehicle parked about one hundred feet away could be seen as the mystery driver began speeding towards us.

"Oh s**t! You wasn't kidding!" Tone responded.

I immediately backed the truck out of the hotel parking lot and headed towards the turnpike exit ramp. Just as I turned the corner to get onto the highway ramp, our aggressor's vehicle collided with us from behind. Drac, who was the only one with his piece in arm's reach, rolled down the back window and began letting off some shots. Two shots were fired towards us and both hit the rear windshield.

"Get down!" I said, driving as fast as I could into oncoming traffic.

We were hit from behind again, and the force of the collision momentarily caused me to steer into the next traffic lane, almost colliding with the highway divider. I also learned the force of the impact caused Drac to lose control of his piece, as it slipped out of his hand and onto the turnpike highway.

Two more gunshots were fired in our direction. One hit my side view mirror. The other, Drac in the same arm he used to fire his weapon. He let out a loud grunt and flopped onto the backseat along with Tone, who had been crouched over in fright since they began firing their shots.

I eventually lost them to my elusive driving skills, but unfortunately not before Drac caught a bad one in the arm. He was bleeding profusely and, from his groans, in a lot of pain. The first thing I had to do was drop off all of the incriminating evidence in the truck and get him some medical attention. After that, I would deal with my pop's connects that had us set up. Like I didn't know that somehow and someway Preemo was the mastermind behind the whole encounter.

CHAPTER NINE

I was in a remote town in West Virginia with my usual following: Tone, Swift, and Drac. It was the first week of May, and the cold weather was finally a thing of the past. With the exception of my recent visit to Georgia, this was the farthest I had ever travelled outside of Brooklyn as the family empire continued to grow. Dealing with my own people had become hazardous to my health. So, Pops hooked me up with some country White folk with more money in their bank accounts than they could ever spend in two lifetimes.

"How much time are you giving us to move this weight?" Tone questioned.

I made a mental note to deal with him later. He knew better than to ask questions in my plain sight that I could easily ask myself. Not exactly insubordination, but something I would deal with when we got back up north nonetheless. Our two country connects, Wild Bob and Bear, took a moment to think about the proposition. Finally, Bear responded in his catchy, southern drawl.

"Exactly thirty days. Yeah, thirty days should suffice. Folks around here tend to get real ornery when they have to wait

David L.

longer than that to get their moolah. Know what I mean?"

"That shouldn't be a problem at all," I responded. "I already have a contract for this stuff. I can have this unloaded in no time."

I was a little ahead of myself and slightly talking out of the side of my mouth, but so what? I had a reputation to uphold. Wild Bob and Bear were both wearing oversized plaid shirts and denim jeans and spitting chewing tobacco. They had on scuffed up Timberland boots, and neither appeared to have shaven in what looked to be well over a month.

As instructed, Swift counted about fifteen Ziploc bags of that white stuff and another twelve bags of marijuana. After everything appeared to match up, Tone proceeded to pay for our product. Nothing but crisp one-hundred-dollar bills were introduced to our connect's pockets.

"You boys been out this way before?" Bear asked.

"Never," I responded. "But if business goes as well as I expect, we'll be making many more trips out this way soon enough."

"We're gonna take good care of you boys while you're here. Call it southern hospitality. That's how we like to do things around these parts."

I've had several run-ins with White folk in the past, and most of them always looked down at me. Maybe not directly like that racist bartender from the diner, but subliminally. To my experience, that's how White folk had always been around me. But, something was different about my two new business associates. Even the way they referred to us as "boys" didn't sound racist coming from them. Not even the slightest bit. I felt very comfortable around them, like we had been doing business for years.

Bear lived up to his promise in ways I could never imagine. The crew and I ate up everything in sight. Bear and Wild Bob even took us out to an all-you-can-eat Chinese buffet, and afterwards, took us out for drinks at a nearby tavern. I thought it was another set-up at one instance when a uniformed cop walked over to us in plain sight. He proceeded to give Wild Bob and Bear a big southern-type hug and then introduced himself to us. Seemed like Innocent wasn't the only one with a crooked cop on the payroll.

"You see that cop that just walked out of here?" Bear questioned.

"Yeah, what about him?" I responded.

"Got him in my back pocket."

"How much?"

"How much what?"

"How much does he charge?"

Bear and Wild Bob let out hearty laughs.

"That there is my people! We grew up together. My mother knows his mother. I ain't got to pay him one red cent."

My monthly payments to a cop that had not come through yet seemed that much more comical in comparison. I could get used to the country life, the quiet and tranquility. More importantly, I would have peace of mind that no one with a reputation to build would put a stray bullet into the back of my head.

Drac, who had never touched liquor in his life, agreed to drive us back home amidst the pleas of Bear and Wild Bob to stay over and hang with them and their boys for at least one more night.

"We have to get back to New York, but you'll see us again real soon. I could learn to live out here," I said.

To further send us off in style, Bear and Wild Bob called on their cop friend to guide us through the back roads and eventually to the highway. Yep. I would definitely be back down to West Virginia because those country folk knew how to treat their guests with style!

David L.

Finally back in New York and ready to go hard on Preemo and his crew, I got an urgent phone call from Tammy. Pop's health had taken a turn for the worse, and Innocent was sent to "the hole" for fighting with another inmate over telephone usage. The hole is where you went when you couldn't function in general population. We met up at Innocent's house, and as usual, my nephew was all over me, kicking and grabbing at my ankles. It had been especially hard on him with his father not being around, and I had privately sworn to look after him as if he was my very own.

"Tammy, calm down. What's going on?"

"Pops will be transferred to intensive care in the morning. He's barely conscious most of the time, and all he does is talk about you and wanting to see you before he leaves us."

"Leave the hospital? And go where?" I responded with obvious naivety.

"Not leave the hospital, you dummy! Leave us as in check out for good. He's getting much worse, and half the time, he slips in and out of consciousness. I don't know how much more time he's got left."

My trip to the hospital was a no-brainer, and the rest of the family and close friends met up with me there, except for Trevor and Angel. Trevor's phone was still turned off, and Angel – well, Angel's phone went straight to voicemail. My return to the hospital reminded me of an earlier visit in which I found out about Angel being pregnant. How ironic I would now return to watch my father as he rapidly deteriorated. Would he even be around to witness his second grandchild be born?

We were directed to a specialized unit in which my pops was now fully conscious and had half the nursing staff in tears. Not tears of sympathy, but tears from laughing so hard. In his earlier days, my pops was a comedian of sorts and always knew how to draw in a crowd with his well-delivered punch lines and uncanny wit.

"Get on in here. Don't be scared, you little punk," he joked, motioning me to give him a hug.

Usually, my father hated showing any displays of emotion, especially in front of other people. He felt it weakened the individual and could be viewed for softness by the opposing enemy. He was putting on a front, but I could tell he was in a weakened state of health. His eyes were sunken into his skull, his complexion was pale, and his skin was cold to the touch.

"I don't have too much time left. You know that right?" he said, looking at me and Tammy.

"Pops don't talk like that. You have to be positive," Tammy responded.

"I am positive. I'm positive the grim reaper will be callin' my name soon!"

He let out a lighthearted chuckle, but neither of us laughed at his weak attempt at humor. Some of the closer members of our family and friends had to wait before coming up to the unit. So, my pops took the time to go over his will with us and explain for what seemed to be the millionth time about how I was in charge of the family business. Pop's estimated worth was rumored to be around three million, so he had his paperwork reviewed over and over again by his legal team.

"I guess no one is going to collect on that bounty on my head," he said meagerly. "Make them pay, son. Make those mutha******* that sent your brother to jail for the rest of his life pay. Promise me."

Then it hit me. My father was facing death and giving it the proverbial finger. He wasn't even concerned that he had been struck down in his middle ages. Instead, he sought revenge for his tormentors. Just looking at my pops in his weakened state had my eyes watery, and I proceeded to excuse myself to the privacy of the restroom. I dare not let Tammy and especially my pops see me like that. Instead, I isolated myself for a few moments and got the tears out the only way I knew – in total seclusion. As I returned to my father's bedside, he was now asleep, and Tammy informed me that before the medication in his I.V. kicked in, he gave her a sealed envelope to give to me.

"Read it out loud. Don't keep me in suspense," Tammy ordered.

I did as requested and was not even the slightest bit shocked at what it said: Don't trust that snake Trevor. I think he had something to do with your brother's set-up.

An hour or so after I left Tammy and my pops at the hospital, I called up the crew and began heading over to the spot where my contracted girls, the Chica Clique, stripped at. While visiting my pops, I had gotten a call from Lord informing me that Preemo was expected to be hanging out at Sonny's that night. I immediately called up Jackie and provided her with all the details and what I expected her to accomplish.

"So can you pull it off?" I questioned.

"Are you going to keep doubting me and my girls' skills?"

"Yeah, I am, until you prove me wrong!"

"Well then, maybe you have the wrong girls working for you!"

We argued back and forth over the phone to the point where I almost rear-ended the car in front of me as I exited the Belt Parkway and proceeded to pick up Tone, Swift, and of course, Drac. Once I got to Sonny's, I was sipping on a cranberry juice waiting for Preemo and his entourage to enter. We were all becoming a little antsy because two more hours dragged by and he had still not arrived. Marisol and Yvonne, two-thirds of the Chica Clique, offered lap dances to Swift and Tone. However, I quickly turned them away. I did not mix business with pleasure, and neither did anyone that worked for me.

"I don't think he's coming tonight. Maybe your boy Lord is pulling a fast one on us and we're the ones being set-up," Tone said.

Tone was again testing me for supremacy and everyone could sense it. Rumor had it that Tone wanted to possibly leave and try the drug game as a soloist. He had better be careful for what he asked for. It's very lonely at the top, and that was assuming he would live long enough to find out.

"We'll give it another fifteen minutes and see what happens," I declared.

Jackie, Marisol, and Yvonne were working the circuit well. All three were extremely beautiful and had a way of enticing even the men with the stingiest of pockets. They were in direct competition with about twenty other strippers, yet they stood out more than any of them under the neon lights. Dollar bill after dollar bill were flying in their direction as they each slid down the nearest stripper pole. The place was packed, the music being played was tolerable, and the free peanuts continued to come in my direction.

Just as I started to get up to leave, Preemo entered the building with whom else: his entourage. Six very big men with scowls on their faces and all of them were wearing full-length, tailor-made suits. All except Preemo, who was wearing a Nike sweat suit and a pair of all-white Air Force One sneakers. Sonny's was crowded to capacity, and I along with everyone else began inhabiting a cozy corner where we could barely be seen by any of the regulars...a spot where hopefully we wouldn't be noticed in.

I motioned for Jackie, who instantly walked off the stage and came over to me.

"That's him right over there. Play into his ego. Gain his trust like you did the other night at the Dynasty Club."

"See, there you go again. Acting like this is a first for me. I got this. Sip on your virgin cranberry and let me do my work."

Tone and Swift got a good laugh at my expense. As usual, Drac just sat in his seat quietly, waiting in anticipation in case something jumped off.

As the night turned to early morning, one by one Preemo's crew went into the back room for what looked to be lap dances by some of the better endowed strippers.

"He hasn't gotten up yet," Swift said, pointing out the obvious.

David L.

"No, but that's okay. Besides, he's here to see Jackie. He's not going to mess that up and walk off with another stripper," I responded.

Sure enough, Jackie finished her pole routine and walked over to see Preemo, who was now ordering a waitress standing behind the bar to bring him over another bottle.

"She's been over there for a minute. You think she's gonna be able to get into his head?" Swift questioned.

Before I had a chance to respond, Preemo left with her to the back room, leaving Marisol and Yvonne behind to work their charm on a couple of his crew that remained by his side.

"Why are we just sitting here eating f**king peanuts and watching everyone else get lap dances? I want a f**king lap dance! You want a lap dance?" Tone asked, looking at Swift. "Besides, we could just have that crooked cop Lincoln roll up on Preemo and his crew and arrest them on the spot! I know they have to be packing guns."

Tone was at it again, trying to test my leadership. No longer would my silence be taken for weakness, but there was not the time. Drac was looking at me for the signal, but I declined, albeit for the time being. The baseball bat to Tone's knee compliments of Drac couldn't have been that much of a distant memory because he was still walking with a noticeable limp and from time to time wore a soft cast on his leg.

"That's not how I do business," I responded. "I'm no snitch, no matter what. I'll get Preemo my way. And Lincoln has enjoyed eating off of me for the last time."

"So we're done messin' with him?" Swift questioned.

"Correct. He's not gonna use our hard-earned funds to put his kids through college anymore. That's my word!"

A few moments went by and Preemo returned to his seat alone. A couple more minutes went by and I got a text from Jackie that read: He will be at my hotel room after I get off...450 Jamaica Avenue...Room 312.

"We got him!" I said with contained emotion.

114

"Got who?" Swift responded.

"Preemo. We got him. He's headed over to Jackie's hotel room after she gets off. It's a done deal!"

"Just like that?"

"Hell yeah, just like that! This mutha****** is gonna get his tonight! That's on my life!"

Content that my plan had finally taken on some resemblance of nearing completion, I sat back in my chair and motioned over a couple of strippers for me and my boys to enjoy. After all, I had a reason to celebrate.

It was a little after three o'clock in the morning, and we were all headed to Queens to confront Preemo, who should have been just arriving at the Motor Inn Motel to see Jackie. I had been texting Jackie back and forth, and she assured me that Preemo had sent his entire crew home. As we pulled up to the Motor Inn, suspicious eyes from behind the motel's customer service desk watched our every move as we headed towards her room. Everything from this point on had been pre-arranged, as Jackie had followed my every instruction with precision and expertise. The room door had been left unlocked so Tone, Swift, Drac, and I could easily enter and catch Preemo off guard. My last text from Jackie let me know he was now lying on the bed in his boxer shorts waiting for her to come out from the bathroom.

"Let's strike," I said in a whisper.

On my command, Drac opened the door, and sure enough, Preemo was sitting up in the bed and caught completely by surprise. Our eyes made contact with one another, and he tried his best to maintain his composure. Simultaneously, Jackie walked out of the bathroom, smiling from ear to ear.

David L.

"So this was a set-up, huh?" Preemo questioned.

"Something like that," I responded.

"Lemme get your gun and put a hole in his head!" Tone said.

We all ignored his infantile outburst and continued on.

"Why did you set my brother up?" I asked him.

"'Cause I was broke off. I got paid very well. Upfront and everything! Normally, I wouldn't go out like that, but it's not every day a brother gets that type of money."

"And it was you that put the bounty on my pops?"

"It was me. Again, the money was too much to pass up."

"What about Innocent's boy Trip? That was you, too?"

"Yeah, but that was for free. Trip owed me for a job that he never paid me for. That was personal between us...strictly personal."

"Yeah, but how did you know he would be at that location?"

"You're kidding me, right? You talkin' about the monthly five thousand drop-off? I knew about that from the jump! My source knew I wanted to get back at Trip and told me that was the best way to go about it. It was a win-win situation for both of us."

I felt like a huge weight had been lifted from my shoulder. All of my questions had been answered. All but one.

"Who paid you? Who wanted to exterminate my family so bad?"

"You'll have to figure that one out for yourself. I tell you, and then I'll have a bounty on my head. Everyone I do business with will think I'm some type of snitch. I'd rather die than go out like that. So, go 'head and take me out of my misery. Handle your business."

Preemo was either one tough son of a b***h or he was bluffing. Either way, I had to get that name out of him. I looked at Drac, and with one well-delivered blow to the back of his head, Preemo was motionless on the ground. Preemo was then gagged and bound with a couple of towels from the bathroom.

"Torture his a**!" I said to Drac.

Jackie pulled out a pocket knife from her purse and handed it to Drac, who then began carving Innocent and my pop's initials into Preemo's skin. We all turned our heads in disgust as Drac continued on with his impromptu artwork.

"Remove the towel from his mouth. Ask him if he's ready to do some talking," I said.

As instructed, Drac shifted the towel, and Preemo immediately had a different outlook on talking to us.

"I'll tell you whatever you want to know!"

"Who paid you?" I questioned.

"You're gonna kill me anyway. No way are you going to let me leave here alive."

"Put the towel back in his mouth and finish carving, Drac!"

"No! I'll tell you!"

"Who?"

"It was your boy Trevor. Don't believe me? Look through my pockets and check my cell phone. Call his number and he will answer. That will prove I'm not lying."

After another look from me, Drac took the pocket knife he used to slice away at Preemo and swung wildly towards his neck, making contact with Preemo's throat and killing him almost instantly. More blood flowed from all directions, and the once white bed sheets were now crimson red.

We quickly exited the motel room, but not before grabbing Preemo's cell phone on our way out.

CHAPTER TEN

*I*t was Sunday at approximately eight o'clock p.m., and the crew and I planned to meet up in front of the Sprint store located in the Bronx for our monthly rendezvous. It was a rainy night, and my new pair of kicks was going to be useless to me after that night. Everyone else was busy complaining about being out there that night in the rain, and both Tone and Swift had already hinted that they wanted to instead go to a nearby Mexican restaurant for some tacos. I had bags under my eyes, and I was yawning from lack of sleep, courtesy of ongoing nightmares of Preemo's very graphic death. Or possibly the guilt that was overcoming me for being directly responsible for the death of another human being. There we met up with my pop's connect "C." I requested a quick transaction so I could surprise Angel over at her apartment and take her out to a late movie and maybe even some much-needed sex afterwards. Looking at all those strippers over at Sonny's the other night had me hornier than I had ever been in my life.

"Yo, C, you need to hook us up with some Blackberry phones," Tone insisted.

C ignored Tone's request and instead went over all the

special functions that came with our new phones.

"Where you headin' to in such a hurry?" Swift questioned.

"I'm stoppin' over by Angel's place. You know how it is," I responded.

"You got all these gold diggers out here chasin' you and you're runnin' behind some broad?" Tone blurted out.

"See, that's exactly why you don't have a girl now," I responded. "You pull all of these fly-by-night chicks from the club and wonder why you can't keep a serious relationship."

I paid C his money for the four cell phones and reminded everyone of what was on the agenda for that weekend. With the purchase of our new merchandise, I signaled my departure and was immediately on my way to Angel's apartment.

Location: 450 Lexington Avenue - Brooklyn. Before I got a chance to get out of my ride, I could detect Angel as she exited her apartment and began walking towards a vehicle parked across the street. It was definitely not her vehicle! No, it was a vehicle being driven by someone I couldn't quite see, but I assumed it was a man because she walked over to the driver's side before getting in and placed a kiss onto his cheek.

"I can't believe this b***h is stepping out on me!" I said to myself in disbelief.

My emotions began to build up even more because, although I have toyed with the idea of creeping in the past, I had never actually followed through with it.

I was too level-headed to act on impulse and step to whoever was driving. Instead, I followed them. Angel knew I was driving my brother's Range Rover, so I had to be extra careful to go unnoticed. A Camry driven by some elderly woman almost caused me to lose them to an upcoming red light that I simply drove through. At last, his car began to slow down, and he eventually pulled into a parking space on St. Johns Avenue. I watched with increased impatience as both of them got out of the car simultaneously, with Angel following him into what appeared to be an apartment building. Out of curiosity, I called Angel again on her cell phone to see if she would look at her phone and acknowledge my call. She did, but then proceeded to place it back into her purse.

"She ain't s**t!"

Angel was carrying my seed, and she was off creeping with the next man. I would have to make her pay, and the best way to do that was to start with her undercover lover. Mental note: 310 St. Johns Avenue. I was looking forward to my return visit to exact some much-needed revenge.

It was too nice of a day to be counting money and reviewing accounting records from inside. So, Drac, Swift, Tone, and I conducted business on the back patio of Innocent's house. Crystal was staying busy barbecuing some steak and beef ribs, and little T.J. was keeping himself busy by playing with the water hose.

"Have you called that number yet?" Tone questioned.

"What number?" I responded.

"From the cell phone. Trevor's number. You didn't call, did you? What are you afraid of?"

My silence was answer enough. However, I refused to come off soft. So, I instructed T.J. to grab the cell phone that was still in the pocket of the pants I wore when we assassinated Preemo at the motel out in Queens not too long ago.

"Let me call," Tone requested.

"No! I got this," was my reply.

"If we're gonna make this work, we should move fast," Swift chimed in.

"Everyone is going to know about Preemo's execution soon enough and try to pin it on us, if they don't know about it already," Tone said.

The number was dialed and a familiar voice answered. It was none other than ex family business associate turned turncoat, Trevor. I immediately hung up and thought about my next course of action. After all, if I were to say anything, Trevor would know I was on to him, and he would also know I was the one that took out his boy. Trevor called back the same cell phone I just called him from, and I let it go directly to voicemail.

"I'm exactly three hundred short on your count," I said, changing the subject back to the task at hand.

Once again, it appeared Tone had come up short with my money. Either he was not counting all of the money when he collected, or he was pocketing some off the top for himself. Either way, I needed to deal with his insubordination immediately the only way I knew how, which was the way I was trained to do so by my brother and Pops.

"Tone, can you explain this? Why is my money not all there?"

"Chill, P. I was gonna re-up. I was trickin' on this chick last night and didn't have money on me, so I dipped in the stash. I can cover it tomorrow when I meet up with a couple of my runners out in Canarsie. Don't even sweat that!"

Swift remained quiet, shaking his head in disbelief. Although he had been very close to Tone, he knew instinctively to never mess with another man's money – no matter what. It was an unwritten code you lived by – or died from. On cue, Drac looked to me and waited for my next directive. But, this was something I had silently decided to handle myself. The combination of hearing Trevor's voice on the other end of the cell phone and my girl cheating had me perplexed.

"Hey, Crystal, are those steaks ready?" I yelled out.

I got up, grabbed a plate, and invited everyone else to do the same. Drac was first and brought his plate back over to the table where we were counting the money. Swift was next, soon followed by Tone.

"Why you lookin' at me like that?" Tone questioned. "I told you that I got you tomorrow."

Tone then proceeded to help himself to the last piece of steak, and I helped myself with a well-placed kick to his injured knee. As Tone bent over in pain, I grabbed him by his neck and shoved him face first into the fiery pit of the BBQ grill. He let out a horrific scream as he collapsed onto the ground. One hand was holding his face and the other, his injured knee. Next, I grabbed the lighter fluid from a nearby table and doused him with it before lighting a match.

"Prentice, STOP!" Crystal screamed. "You'll kill him! T.J., go into the house! NOW!"

"Get him the f**k out of here, Drac! And tell him to have my money by tomorrow morning. Nine a.m. on the dot! "

"What about Trevor?" Swift asked.

"Here, take the phone. Send him a text."

"And say what?"

"He's gonna think it's from Preemo. So, ask him to meet up with us to talk business."

"Where?"

"I don't know. Anywhere. No, I know. Tell him in front of the Ice Cream Factory on Nostrand Avenue."

"And then what?"

"Then we meet him there. If he comes by himself, then he doesn't know yet about what happened to Preemo."

"And if he comes with backup?"

"Then he knows Preemo is dead and we are being set up. Either way, we'll have the jump on him. Set it up for later this afternoon and call the girls up. We may need them there to run some interference while we figure out how to get him."

Nostrand Avenue. A section of Brooklyn that I didn't have any stake in and that was notorious for gang activity and drug-related shootings. Many Haitian, Jamaican immigrants, and first generationers populated this area, and often shot first and asked questions later.

"See those young boys over there on their bikes in front of the Ice Cream Factory?" I said to Swift.

"Yeah, what about them?"

"I got them on the payroll. Their names are Marley and Fredro. The same two stick-up kids that beat your boy Tone out of my loot."

"What are they out here for?"

"They are runnin' interference for us. Jackie is already inside. She knows what she needs to do."

"What are those kids gonna do for us but get in the way?"

"Watch for yourself."

As expected, Trevor rolled up by himself in a cab and got out from the passenger side. That may have meant he had someone waiting nearby to pick him up. I couldn't be too sure, so I decided to wait patiently instead. He was now looking around, probably for me. Drac couldn't make the trip with Swift and I because one of his children had to be rushed to the emergency room. So, I was already outmanned in case anything popped off.

"Okay, here it comes. Watch this," I said.

Right on cue, my young stick-up crew knocked an old lady down in broad daylight and took off with her purse. Fredro shoved her to the floor and Marley grabbed her purse. Both rode off in different directions on their bikes.

"What did they do that for?" Swift questioned.

"Think about it. If that dirty cop was nearby, he probably would've pursued them, don't you think?"

"Or he could always just radio it in to someone else to deal with them."

"Well, that's a chance I'm gonna have to take."

"Okay, that explains those two young boys. What about Jackie, though? What good is she to us right now?"

"After that job she pulled for us out in Queens, you really wanna ask me that question? She's gonna do what she does best. Watch and learn!"

I really had no idea what was being said between Jackie and Trevor, who was now inside and looked to be ordering something. I was slowly developing a renewed confidence for Jackie's skills, so I didn't bother to text her with any more updates. If I were a betting man, I would say she was getting into Trevor's head. Besides, what would I have proven by walking up to Trevor in broad daylight and shooting him? Lincoln may not have been around, but who was to say he didn't have someone else lurking and watching his back. Bad boys move in silence, and I knew very well how to play my position.

"Let's go," I said to Swift as I drove off. "Jackie can fill me in later."

A half hour later, I got a text that simply read: Where are you? I waited for you for over thirty minutes.

"What are you smiling about?" Swift questioned.

I showed him the text and plotted my next course of action.

"He doesn't yet know about Preemo," I responded. "That means we got him. Checkmate!"

With my brother fresh out of the hole in Elmira Correctional Facility, I was finally able to take the long ride up to visit him. He had lost a few pounds, grew a beard, and appeared slightly more humbled than his usual arrogant self. I guess that's what thirty days of isolation does to a man who was used to doing anything he wanted when he was out in the streets. This time, I

David L.

was also accompanied by my brother's longtime friend and enforcer, Drac. As usual, he played the background and allowed my brother and me to catch up on old times. As expected, I tried to talk about pleasant memories and family, whereas Innocent wanted to keep everything strictly business related.

"I got a visit from the lettermen," Innocent said.

The "lettermen" was slang for anyone that worked for the FBI, CIA, or DEA.

"What did they come see you for?" I responded.

"Preemo's death, that's what. You took him out, but you were sloppy. My initials were carved into him. Mine and Pops."

"Those could've been anyone's initials," I said meagerly.

"Boy, don't play with me! Them FBI chumps were down here grilling me for over an hour."

"My fault. It's just that I wanted to send a message and let them know that just 'cause you're locked away don't mean you can't pull some strings from in here. It won't happen again. That's my word."

"They tried to get me to talk. They're probably gonna be talking to Pops and you, as well. Let him know he should probably stay out in Connecticut for the time being. Don't be out runnin' in the streets for at least a couple of weeks until things die down a little."

And then it hit me. Innocent didn't know about Pop's condition. He didn't know Pops did not have too much time left.

"Yo, Innocent – about Pops…"

"Don't even go there, kid," he interrupted. "I knew this wasn't what you had planned, but you stepped up your game. You stepped up like a mutha******! Between Pops and I putting the pressure on you, and always tryin' to get you mixed up with our s**t, you finally came around on your own. Pops may never say it, kid, but he's proud of you. We all are. So what about Pops you wanted to tell me?"

"Nothing. Forget about it."

I shifted the conversation back to business. Innocent had

126

just came out from a place where he had no human contact whatsoever. No one to talk to. No books or magazines to read. I didn't need to add to his problems by telling him how serious our father's condition had progressed. I did, however, inform him of his boy Trevor. The look of disbelief on his face was obvious, as I was instructed to tell him everything I knew from Lincoln, the dirty cop, getting set up in New Jersey to Preemo's confession before we ended his life. Then and only then was he convinced of Trevor's treachery and ordered a hit out on him through me.

"Already done, big brother. Trevor may as already be dead, because his time is limited."

"Be careful, kid. He's smart, and he's got cops in his pocket. You don't think Lincoln is the only one out there, do you? Lincoln is one of many. Get your entire team in place and strike now. He knows you will be coming for him and will try to take you out first."

Innocent was not eligible for another visit for another thirty days from me, or anyone else for that matter. It would not take me that long to have some good news for him when I returned.

Innocent was right about the lettermen coming to pay me a visit. Two of them were parked in an unmarked vehicle right as I pulled up to the curb in front of Innocent's house. The same neighbor that gave us the license plate information from earlier in the year was looking out from his window and quickly closed his curtains when he saw me look over in his direction. So what do I do? I invited them in. Besides staying at Innocent's house and helping out with the day-to-day needs of his baby's mother and his only son, what could they connect to me? Absolutely nothing.

"So what can I do for you, gentlemen?" I questioned.

"Don't be so formal, Prentice. I'm Special Agent Johnson and my partner here is Special Agent Samuels. We would like to ask you a few questions."

"A few questions, huh? Okay. Ask."

T.J., with his usual inquisitive personality, walked over to us to see what we were talking about.

"Hey there, little man. You look just like the picture we have of your father," Johnson said.

I immediately grabbed T.J. and redirected him back to his room before either one of them had a chance to shake his hand or ask him any questions.

"What would make a bright fellow like you with the rest of his life ahead of him want to drop out of school?" Samuels asked.

"I took some time off. That's all."

"Time off? Who takes time off in the middle of a semester? You paid for twelve credits of schooling, didn't you? That's a lot of money!"

"I had some family problems. Family comes first where I'm from."

"Exactly around the time your brother got put away for the rest of his life," Johnson added. "That's one helluva coincidence."

"So what are you implying?"

"That you're mixed up with your brother...and your father. We know all about him, as well. They put you on to continue their drug empire because he's not in the best of health, is he?"

"I don't know what you're talking about. I'm done talking!"

It may have sounded like Johnson and Samuels were getting under my skin, but that's what I wanted them to think. Truth be told, I was actually getting a laugh watching their rendition of a "good cop, bad cop" routine. Then, out of the blue, I was asked a question by Johnson that captured my interest.

"You know anything about either your brother or father

getting involved with any crooked cops?"

Reverse psychology or genuine interest? Either way, I was not talking about anything. I messed up when I allowed Drac to go overboard with Preemo's death. I was not going to say anything to implicate anyone, even a dirty rat bastard like Lincoln.

"Nah, I don't know anything about any dirty cops."

"Yeah, that's what your brother said. I can tell now why the two of you are related," Johnson remarked.

With nothing more to get out of me, both Johnson and Samuels handed me a business card and asked that I keep in touch if the need arose. Then they departed, leaving me with even more questions.

With a few hours to kill, I called up Drac and told him to wait for me as I exited Innocent's home to go pick him up. Our destination: 310 St. Johns Avenue. We got over there pretty quickly. The blue Maxima that I followed behind a few nights ago was in front of the same apartment I travelled to previously. So, I assumed the one I was looking for was at home, or maybe Angel was there as an added bonus. I would love to see the look of embarrassment on her face as I cold bust her in front of her lover. That would have been double the fun.

"We got business over here that I don't know about?" Drac asked.

"Nothing like that," I replied. "But, I do have something of a personal nature to deal with while I'm here. This has to be a fair one. So, unless there is more than one person occupying the apartment, let me handle what I need to handle."

I didn't have the slightest clue as to which apartment was his, but I had four doors to choose from. So, I decided to ring all of the bells in the apartment building. Two of the doorbells had female names attached to the bottom sticker, so that increased my probability of guessing the correct one. I got it right on my first attempt. The brother, who goes by Dayvon, opened the door and looked startled to see me and Drac looking him in the

David L.

eyes.

"What's up? You're Angel's man, right? We met the other night."

"What's up is you're f**king my girl! And you looked me right in my mutha****ing face in her apartment and shook my hand!"

"It's not even like that," was his meager reply. "We're just friends."

"Yeah, it's exactly like that."

No more time for words, I forced myself into his apartment and threw a wild haymaker that Dayvon elusively dodged. He followed with a wild haymaker of his own in obvious self defense that barely connected. I could sense Drac stepping forward, and instead, I requested that he close the door behind us and stay out of my one-on-one.

"Yo, we don't have to do this!" Dayvon insisted.

I didn't respond. Instead, I picked up the nearest weapon of choice within arm's reach: his lamp. I swung it towards his head, but he crouched down and took out my legs from under me. Now we were rolling around on the floor trying to get the best of one another. He was the first to connect with a solid blow to my temple and another which barely grazed my cheek. I followed through with a right to his jaw. He had me in height, but I could tell I had him in the strength department.

"Are we seriously fighting over a woman? How weak is that?" he said to me.

My rage intensified for two reasons. One, I couldn't lose this fight in front of Drac, or in front of anyone for that matter. Two, Dayvon was one hundred percent correct. If I had to come out here to confront this clown, then Angel was never really mine to begin with, whether she was carrying my seed or not.

I came to my senses and put my hands down, signaling my decision to end an altercation towards an individual who was only doing what came natural. Like the old saying goes: a man is going to be a man. I knew Drac was always strapped while

130

outdoors, so I walked over to him so he could hand me his piece.

"You're gonna shoot me?" Dayvon questioned. "Don't do this!"

"No, I'm not gonna shoot your punk a**. I'm not even going to play myself like that. But, you're right about fighting over that cheatin' b***h!"

"So why you got your gun pointed in my direction?"

"Because if I ever see you again, I'm going to put a hole in your skull. You understand me?"

"Yeah, I understand. You will never see me again. You can count on it. Angel won't see my Black a** again either!"

On that note, Drac and I departed Dayvon's apartment, all the while knowing I was eventually going to get clowned about tonight from both Tone and Swift, and possibly everyone else in the crew.

CHAPTER ELEVEN

I was awakened by the sound of my cell phone ringing. It was my sister Tammy and she was hysterical with obvious grief.

"This can't be good," I said under my breath.

Just like I predicted, it wasn't. There's never good news at almost four o'clock in the morning.

"Pops is dead," Tammy uttered. "I just got the phone call from the hospital."

"DAMN!"

My heart dropped, and I asked her to repeat herself with the unlikely possibility that I was only having a bad dream. I was not. I wasn't the least bit surprised because we all had been expecting it to happen sooner or later, but I always privately felt that my pops would survive his dreaded illness. Somehow, I always envisioned my father passing away with all of us around his death bed, telling jokes to us no less.

"I'll be right down to the hospital," I said.

I immediately awakened both Crystal and T.J. and then warmed up the truck. Next, I sent Angel a text to let her know what had happened. Not that I thought she would respond anyway. As expected, upon my arrival, Tammy was even more hysterical and crying so loudly that a couple of the nursing staff had to remind her that there were other patients trying to sleep. "I don't give a damn about your patients! My father is dead!" I overheard Tammy saying to one of the orderlies.

One of my aunts, who had travelled all the way from Florida to be at his side, was doing her best to console Tammy, but with no success.

For the first time in years, my pops looked to be at peace. No more worries about any bounties on his head, the Feds looking to put him away for the rest of his life, or worrying that he would somehow because of the lives we lead, outlive one of his offspring. He could finally get some rest. Maybe even rekindle his relationship with my mother in the hereafter. Yes, he was definitely in a better place for the first time in his life.

"Look who's here," Crystal said, motioning me to turn around.

It was Angel. Besides Drac, Crystal was the only other person I had told about her cheating a** ways. I could hardly stand to look at her. However, that was not the time. So, I decided to do the mature thing instead.

"I didn't think you would make it out here," I said.

"Don't go there, Prentice. That's your father you're talking about. I know how much you loved and respected him. There's no way I would miss coming here."

I would never tell my crazy a** sister about Angel's infidelity because she never liked her anyway. Knowing my sister, she would have probably slapped her right there in front of everyone. When T.J. came over to try and give Angel a hug, I motioned for him to go back over to his mother instead. I didn't care if that was my baby she was carrying; I was so through with her. Even though all I should have been thinking about was my pop's passing, I had more contempt in my heart for Angel at that moment than grief.

"I know about you and that clown that was over your

apartment for your birthday. And I can tell from the look on your face that you know that I know. How could you?"

Before things could get heated, Crystal wisely recommended that we take our conversation into the waiting area.

"How could I, Prentice? You chose this lifestyle over me, remember? Over your unborn child, as well."

"Stop it. You're talkin' like you're straight out of a soap opera! And how do I know that's even my child in there? Maybe that baby belongs to the guy that got his a** beat and almost s**t in his pants! Oh, you better believe I'm gonna be asking for a blood test."

"You can do anything you want, Prentice, but this child I'm carrying is yours. And whether or not you choose to be in his or her life...well, that's entirely up to you."

Even though both of us departed to the waiting area to talk in privacy, we were anything but quiet. In fact, we were so loud that hospital security was eventually called on us by one of the orderlies and we were requested to leave the hospital.

Feelings aside, the code of the streets told me that I needed to take my losses like a man and never deal with her trifling, cheating a** again...but my heart said differently. I would have to deal with those matters of the heart another day.

When word finally got out about my pop's passing, there were going to be a lot of unhappy individuals who either had made a lot of money from their dealings with him or who had their heart set in collecting on that one hundred thousand dollar bounty.

It was payday, or at least that's what Lincoln thought. I received an anonymous text a few moments beforehand for us to meet up at the same diner we met up at before. I promised myself he would be cut off for good. So what did I do? I called up the troops, of course. Everyone except Tone responded. However, we still managed to beat Lincoln to the spot.

"So how much does he want now?" Swift questioned.

"Six thousand a month!"

"Damn! Now he wants six? Before it was five. Next month it will be seven. His price is just gonna go up until we do something about it. And what has he done for us? He hasn't done anything yet, and we're still paying him? F**k that!"

"Exactly! He's about to be in for a rude awakening," I responded.

I neglected to tell Drac and Swift that I received a visit from the lettermen a few nights ago. I would have been very surprised if they didn't have someone tailing me and watching my every move. That may have worked to my advantage in the long run.

"So are you ready for the repercussions when you tell him that he's no longer getting paid?" Drac questioned.

"I'm ready for whatever. Let him bring it!"

Bravado aside, I was slightly inquisitive about how Lincoln would react when I straight refused to pay him any longer. Or if he would make any random comments about what happened to Preemo at the motel out in Queens. But, I had no time to worry about that when I saw him pulling up to the rear of the diner.

"Good afternoon, gentlemen," he said with a smug smile on his grill. "I'm taking the wife to some dumb play she's been dying to go to for some time now, so let's make this quick."

"It's gonna be real quick," I responded. "'Cause you ain't getting nothin' from us. You're cut off! Your services are no longer needed!"

Lincoln's smug smile turned into a scowl. From the corner of my eye, I could see a couple of waitresses who appeared nervous about coming over to our table. I could hear them arguing about which one should come over and take our order.

"You sure about that, Prentice Barnes, Innocent Junior, or whatever they call you out here in these streets? You don't want to get on my bad side, boy. Trust me on this one."

"F**k you, pig!" I blurted out. "We got a new rule about giving away hard-earned cash to individuals who try to muscle us."

He was now leaning over in his seat, visibly perplexed. He was trying his best to get under my skin by bringing my brother into the conversation, but no dice. I was better than that. I had my head on straight that day.

"You're a glorified beat cop, Lincoln," I responded. "You're a nobody! Get this through your head...you are cut off from this moment on. You will never see another dime from me again. Not as long as I live! Got it? Tell the wife I said hello."

"Well, if that's the way you want it. Have it your way, boys."

With nothing more to say, Lincoln removed himself from the table and left the diner. All of that bravado had left me famished, and I took the time to order some takeout for the ride back home. The waitress that lost the argument eventually came over, and although I was a little perturbed about the time it took for my order, I still proceeded to leave her a generous tip. If she ever saw me again in that diner, my guess is she would be more than willing to take care of my order in a timely fashion.

Less than half a mile past the diner after paying my bill, flashing lights alerted me to the fact that I was being signaled to pull over.

"You got anything in the truck?" Swift asked.

"No, I'm clean, and so is Drac. I had a feeling something like this may happen."

"So where are you boys headed?" a cop questioned.

He had the same smug smile Lincoln had in the diner not too long ago. About two to three minutes later, another cop car pulled up to where we were pulled over.

"I'm on my way home," I responded. "Why?"

"So what's the real reason you pulled us over?" Swift asked.

"It sure can't be 'cause I was driving too fast, 'cause I was following the speed limit," I added.

"Get out the car," the cop commanded.

Doing as instructed, all three of us were spread eagle against the hood of my ride. Traffic behind us and on the opposite side was beginning to slow down almost to a halt just so they could go home and tell their loved ones about the three Black men that were pulled over on the side of the road.

"So how long before you and your partner plant some drugs in the vehicle?" I questioned.

"You watch too many movies, boy," the cop responded. "Put your hands where I can see them! And don't make any sudden movements."

There is that word again: boy. He must have been down with Lincoln. He didn't have to worry about me making any sudden movements. From the look on his grill, he was probably only too eager to put a bullet in me. It would be just one more dead n***a to write up about at the end of his shift.

"That's not what we're about, but you're going to take a ride downtown for questioning. Don't worry about your ride. A tow truck will be here shortly to tow your shiny ride to a nice, safe place."

Drac was escorted into a squad car by himself, probably because of his large frame. Swift and I were handcuffed and placed in the other squad car. Just as we were driven off to the precinct, a familiar looking car could be seen from a distance double-parked. I was almost certain the vehicle belonged to Lincoln. Too much of a coincidence not to be his. He was probably seated behind his steering wheel, sipping on a coffee and laughing hysterically to himself over our unfortunate predicament.

My cuffs were on extra tight, and when I asked for them to be loosened, I was laughed at and told to shut my mouth. Down at the police station, the three of us were immediately separated for questioning. More good cop, bad cop nonsense that we had all been trained on extensively by my father before he passed. The rules were simple: keep a straight face at all times and say nothing that can implicate anyone from the crew. No fingerprints were ever taken. No rights were ever read to us. Nothing.

Swift, Drac, and I were then placed in a holding cell together and left by ourselves for a little over an hour.

"This is some bull****!" Tone said.

"You think Lincoln is behind this?" Drac questioned.

"Don't say nothing. This cell is probably bugged," I said. "That's why they have us up in here together."

My warning to Swift and Drac were the last words uttered in that holding cell until a uniformed officer came in and released us from our handcuffs. Then we were led into a semi-dark room with nothing but a couple of chairs and an old wooden table on which someone left an empty can of soda.

"Wait in here," the officer said. "Someone will be with you in a few minutes."

That "someone" was none other than Lincoln. He was sporting that same signature smile that he had on his face from the diner.

"So, boys, are you ready to talk business? Or do we have to go through this every f**king day until you realize you can't win against me?"

The ball was now in his court and he knew it. Deep down, I knew anything could have happened that day instead of just being brought down to the station. We could've been beaten...or worse. He knew it, and more importantly, he knew that we knew it. None of his cohorts were around, but the slightest movement or smart comment by any of us and only GOD knew what would happen next. I spoke with great deliberation, making sure I spoke for both myself and those I represented.

"Yeah, let's talk business," I responded.

Lincoln increased his going rate by another grand for what he considered arrogance and insubordination on my part. After I feigned acceptance, we all left the precinct, but not before calling a cab to take us to where the Range had been towed.

"Yo, we gotta fix him," Swift said, stating the obvious.

"Don't worry. We will. Matter of fact, I want him so bad, I'm willing to hold off getting Trevor!"

"So now we got a hit out on a cop?" Drac asked.

"That could be suicide on our part," Swift added.

"Could be, but we're already dead if we allow him to get away with this. If you wanna pull out and get out the game, I understand. Is that what you want?"

"No, I'm in."

"So, then, let's get the girls together as well as my young guns, Marley and Fredro. If we're gonna go all out, we're going to have to act quickly before Lincoln can figure out what's happening."

My father's funeral service looked more like a BET awards show because of all the high-rollers and big-time individuals that stopped through to pay their respects. Everyone from the low-level lookout man to the major drug traffickers stopped by, if even momentarily to give their condolences to a man they both admired and feared. People from all across the five boroughs and beyond arrived to show my family love on this dark day – including Trevor. I nudged Tammy from where I was seated and informed her of the traitor in our midst.

"He's probably trying to get you to do something reckless," she said. "Don't do anything here."

"Do I look stupid?" I responded. "But, he's got a lot of balls showing up here today."

The rest of the crew also got my attention in order to alert me of Trevor's arrival. If I didn't walk over to where he was standing, it would look suspicious. So, I did just that. I motioned for Drac to remain seated and let me talk with Trevor by my lonesome.

"My only wish would be that they allowed my brother to attend the service," I said to Trevor, giving him a hug. "By the way, have you been by to see Innocent?"

"Not yet, but I promised myself to make it out there before the end of the summer," he responded.

"You change your cell number? I've been tryin' to reach you for some time now, but your phone was cut off."

"Yeah, I changed my cell number a while ago. I had given out my number to so many chicks that it was beginning to catch up to me. I almost got busted by wifey! Remind me to get you the number before we break out of here."

"Okay, I'll do that. By the way, I had a run-in with your boy Lincoln. He went as far as having me set up by some of his boys in blue after I told him that I wasn't paying him his loot any longer."

"Yeah, I heard about that. Don't worry about Lincoln. I'll straighten everything out with him. He won't be messin' with you after I have a talk with him."

I could smell the lies seeping out of Trevor's pores. He was a damn good liar, but a liar nonetheless. I listened in disbelief as he even went as far as to quote a scripture from the Bible to reflect on my pop's life and give his well wishes for me and my family. Whether or not he knew about Preemo yet was still uncertain. He was playing it cool, as did I.

From the corner of my eye, I could see two recognizable individuals standing on the opposite end of the back area of the funeral parlor as they waved me over. I reluctantly obliged and informed Trevor I would get up with him after the service so we could reconnect and exchange cell phone numbers.

"What are you two doing here?" I questioned. "Can't you

just let my father rest in peace and leave me the hell alone?"

The two individuals were the same lettermen that paid me a visit last week: Special Agents Johnson and Samuels.

"We're here for you," Johnson said.

"For me? What can you possibly do for me?"

"I know you think you're all big and bad and you got your little posse taking orders for you, but…"

"Let me stop you right there. I'm not big or bad, and what posse are you referring to? My family? Some of my friends that I've known since I was a kid?"

"Yeah, whatever. Play dumb if you want, but you have a price on your head, as well. And your friend standing over there is the one that's planning to collect on it."

"Who? Trevor? I'm not worried about him."

"You need to be. He's established. You're a replacement for your brother."

"We're done talking. Enjoy the rest of your day."

"You still have my card?"

"I think so, but I make it a point not to converse with the Feds."

"Here, take it again. Use it. It may save your life."

They both departed as inconspicuous as they arrived. Just in time, as I was called up to the altar to give some farewell words in dedication to my fallen father.

Outside of the church, all of our family huddled around one another for a silent prayer in tribute to Forrester "Crime" Mitchell - my father. My sister's loser boyfriend and soon-to-be fiancé surprisingly showed up just as the service was coming to an end. They walked off somewhere for privacy to more than likely argue about something probably very trivial and unimportant. Swift and Drac walked over in my direction, and once again, there was no sign of Tone. It was now clearly obvious he had been missing in action since the day at Innocent's backyard in which I had to teach him a lesson in humility.

"So what did Trevor have to say?" Swift questioned. "Don't keep me hangin'."

"Forget about that. Have you spoken to Tone? He's been M.I.A. for a minute now. He's your partner, right? Y'all used to be inseparable, so you gotta know something."

"On the real, Tone is wildin'. He says he can't be down with you and recently began working for himself. I've been meaning to talk to you about that."

"No big deal. He was a liability anyway, and how long do you think he's gonna last in these streets with no back-up? By the way, congratulations!"

"For what?"

"I've been meaning to tell you...you're my new lieutenant. You accept?"

"Hell f**king yeah! Good lookin' out!"

Trevor made his way over to us, and as promised, he gave me his cell phone number. From memory, I could tell it wasn't the same number I called him on while using Preemo's cell phone.

All of the guests and grieving women in my pop's life were walking slowly out of the church. Some of the women he was having relations with were standing together in front of a big oak tree and looked to be comparing stories of their dealings with him. Another identifiable face began to walk over to me. Behind him were my sister and her boyfriend. The identifiable face belonged to one of my father's trusted business associates: Abe Rothstein, his lawyer of many years.

"I've got a letter to give to the two of you," he said, referring to my sister and me. "It's of a private nature."

I immediately requested Tammy's boyfriend to excuse himself, which he smartly did...however, not without some reluctance. Abe then pulled out an envelope from his briefcase and handed it to Tammy to read out loud. It was the last letter my father ever wrote in confidence. His plan was to give it to my sister and me, but fate had other plans.

David L.

If the two of you are reading this, then I have already crossed over to a better place. I've made a lot of money in my life, but I've also made a lot of mistakes. Even more importantly, I've made a lot of enemies. You may want to reconsider your involvement with our family business. I have a son who is doing life in prison and another who will undoubtedly also end up in jail or worse – dead like I am. Look after your sister, Prentice. She is my only girl and my heart. Protect her from those that will use her as leverage to get back at me – or Innocent. Learn from my mistakes. If not, you will be condemned to repeat them. I'm with your mother now. Don't feel pity for me or grieve my absence, for I am now truly at peace.

With his job now done, Abe closed up his briefcase and bid us both a farewell. My sister was teary-eyed, and I was left holding my father's last letter in utter shock and disbelief. He wanted me to retire? My father and to a lesser extent my brother were the reasons I'm the man that I am today.

One thing was for sure. Like it or not, those FBI men and I had some catching up to do. My life may very well have depended on it.

CHAPTER TWELVE

reenwich, Connecticut. Abe Rothstein suggested I stop by my father's house for additional information, so I did just that. Along for the ride were my sister Tammy, Drac, and Swift. Either my father was getting very paranoid before his passing because of the bounty on his head, or he had serious insight into who wanted to see his family empire come to a screeching halt. We arrived to the house in a little over one hour, and a mid-forties looking White woman came to the door and received us with open arms.

"I've been expecting you," she said with great emotion. "Your father's lawyer told me that you might be stopping by to look through some of his belongings. I feel like I know you already from the many times Forrester talked about you. Come on in the house. I just finished cooking. Your father loved my cooking!"

We all gathered in what looked to be a den of sorts. There were so many rooms in my father's mansion that one could not be quite sure. One thing that stood out in my father's home was that there were no pictures of us on the walls or anywhere else. No sign of the fact that he had a family of any kind. The mansion itself was huge. Six bedrooms, three and a half bathrooms, a study hall, den, and a guest house in the back. His kitchen was the largest I had ever seen, and as I opened the refrigerator door, the top shelf was filled to capacity with bottled spring water and dozens of low-fat yogurt. For all the times my father had talked about his house, I had never been there to visit. Neither had Tammy and we were both regretful for that.

"What was your relationship with my pops?" Tammy questioned. "He's never mentioned you before."

"That's just like Forrester to leave out the many details of his life. He and I were very serious up until his passing. We met at the mayor of Connecticut's birthday bash a little over a year ago. We were planning on flying out to the Virgin Islands on Christmas weekend to tie the knot. It was going to be a surprise. Then he fell ill. I miss him so much, but I know he's still here in spirit."

Tammy consoled my pop's fiancé, while I took that rather awkward moment to start searching the rest of the house. Drac and Swift were in awe at the sheer size of each room, and both promised that before they left the drug game, they would have a mansion that could compare with that one. Hopefully, both of my partners would be alive to one day see their dreams come true.

"Did my father have any secret locations or safes of any kind that you know about?" I asked. "And please accept my apologies because I don't even know your name."

She introduced herself as Carol and walked me over to another room in the house. After filling their stomachs with Carol's home-baked brownies, Drac and Swift accompanied me into the next room.

"What exactly are we looking for?" Swift questioned. "It's gonna take us a million years to look through every room in this house."

"It's not how long you look, it's where you look," I

responded.

"Well then, let's begin so we can get this over with."

"I'm not quite sure where to begin to tell you the truth. Abe hinted my father may have stashed away some additional letters that may lead me in the direction of what went down between him and Trevor."

"What makes you think something went down between the two of them?"

"'Cause he wrote me a note when I visited him in the hospital stating I should not trust Trevor."

"And that's what you're basing this off of? No offense, P, but your pops was on his way out. He was probably delirious or something."

"My father was anything but delirious. I still have the note in my book bag. He was very clear about his suspicions of Trevor."

Swift, Drac, and I spent over an hour looking through my pop's dresser drawers and searching for hidden compartments in each room we entered. Still, we had not covered half of my father's house. Tammy preoccupied herself by keeping Carol company and out of our way so we could search in privacy.

"Do you think she even knows about what Crime did for a living?" Swift questioned.

"I don't think so," was my reply. "My pops usually kept his lady friends out of the loop. He felt women didn't have a place in our business dealings. Even my moms, who knew of everything that went down, was relegated to playing the background when it came to my pop's affairs."

"She was more than a lady friend," Drac added. "Dude was gonna marry that chick. She said it herself."

"My pops get married again? Yeah, right! My pops was probably just pumpin' her head up. Getting into that poor White woman's head...and her pockets!"

Outside in the yard, a Hispanic-looking man was doing garden work and emptying garbage into a large recycle bin. You could tell he was hard at work because every few seconds, he stopped momentarily to wipe his brow of the sweat from the scorching sun that was directly above him.

"Who is he?" I asked Carol.

"Who? Manuel? He's been cleaning up your father's yard for as long as he's had this house. He's sort of a jack-of-all-trades. He does plumbing, electrical work, paints...you name it."

"So he does indoor and outdoor work for my pops?"

"Sure. Would you like to meet him?"

I obliged and Manuel was called into the house. He was sweating profusely, and I promised him not to take up too much of his time.

"You know my pop's house pretty good?" I asked.

"I know your pop's house inside and out. Why do you ask?"

"'Cause I'm looking for some letters he may have written. Did he have a favorite part of the house he used to write in, or go to be by himself?"

"Often I would see him sitting in his car in the garage not doing much. Just sitting there in deep thought."

"Anything else I may need to know?"

"No, I don't think so. Whenever he was home, he spent the majority of his time either in his den...or in the garage. He enjoyed his private time."

I thanked him for his time and got back to my search. Swift and Drac wanted to end the search and return to Brooklyn, and Tammy was busy talking Carol's ear off with her own wedding plans for the future. Before we headed back to Brooklyn, I proposed that we make one last ditch attempt and search my pop's garage for any clues. There was nothing much in the garage itself. However, several folded up letters were found in the glove compartment of one of his cars. It was a collector's edition Trans Am that he had not driven in over a decade. Jackpot! There were about ten letters hidden way in the back of the glove compartment, and between Swift, Drac, and myself, we quickly read through each of them in no time. One letter in particular gave much clearer insight into Trevor's reason for treachery.

"What you got there?" Drac questioned.

"Listen to this. My father actually kept a journal that he wrote in just about every day."

March 3rd. Trevor and I met up in the Bronx at our usual spot to discuss his role in the family business and eventually being second-in-command upon my retirement. I denied his request, and his anger and disappointment was evident. My loyalty to him and the years he put in to build the family name was questioned, and he immediately stormed out the bar. He later sent me a text apologizing for his outburst and said he understood my reasoning for continuing in my efforts to include my youngest son in the family business.

"Damn! So that's why Trevor switched sides," I said in astonishment.

"Don't blame yourself," Drac said

"I don't. Not in the least. But it does explain a lot."

Innocent's Range Rover had been prematurely put to rest... an early retirement of sorts. That was what usually happened when one was pulled over by corrupt cops on a payroll five times in just as many days. Although I had indicated to Lincoln that money would be due as promised, he was trying to prove a point at my expense. Or maybe he was just taking his orders from Trevor.

That was what prompted me to go out and purchase a new 2010 silver Dodge Charger with all the extras. It was turbo-charged and full of horsepower. The very next night, we planned to bring it to Lincoln for all the trouble he had been putting me and my family through. Me, Drac, and Swift rolled up to Fort Greene Park to meet up with Lord and Wise for a little last-minute rendezvous, which would go down as a win-win situation for all of us.

"You trust those two?" Swift questioned.

"I don't trust anyone. But, I have to follow my instincts on this one. So far, Lord and Wise came through for me, so I'm gonna give them the benefit of the doubt…at least for the time being."

Swift and I were referring to a connect that had been pre-arranged. We were to all meet up at the park to discuss some potential narcotic runs back and forth to Hartford, Connecticut with a couple of Dominican cats that resided there. They preferred to do business with their own kind. So, I quickly called up my ace in the hole, Jackie, to meet up with us at the park and translate if necessary. I was uncharacteristically late since I had to drive across town to pick Jackie up from the strip club. At Fort Greene Park, Lord and Wise arrived exactly as we were parking.

"Where are your connects?" I questioned.

As usual, Lord did most of the talking. And as usual, he was dressed down and looking like he was getting ready to play basketball instead of make a deal.

"They'll be here. I've only been working with them for about a month, but they look to be on point. And their money is long!"

The aura of arrogance that Lord once displayed towards me seemed to be not as evident as in the past. Although we were in competition by nature, we did our dirt in different areas. Thus, there was no reason to clash. At least not yet anyway.

"Here they are now," Wise interrupted.

Two Dominican cats rolled up in a pimped-out Yukon Denali, wearing shades and blazers in the summertime, looking like they were straight out of *Miami Vice*. The overall contract was simple enough, however ingenious for time-management purposes. Neither Lord nor I wanted to work with that much weight for one contract. So, he had graciously agreed to spread the wealth. I couldn't fault him for that. On alternating months, my crew and Lord's crew would take turns transporting three kilos of coke to an abandoned warehouse in Hartford. Once there, we would be greeted by one of their own who would hand us sixty thousand dollars in cash – all in twenty-dollar bills. Why all twenties? Because money in low denominations was easier to spread around in the street. No one wanted to be flashing century notes anymore – at least that's what we were told.

Our two Dominican connects appeared antsy and spent a lot of time looking over their shoulders. No product was exchanged that day; however, another mutually agreed upon meeting was expected to take place very soon so that my crew could take over the next Connecticut run. After they both departed to make the long ride home, I took the opportunity to dig for some more information from Lord.

"Good lookin' out on that Preemo hook up," I said, referring to earlier information that allowed Jackie to get close enough to do her job. Speaking of which, Lord made it visibly known that he had his eye on her. However, she was not giving him the time of day.

"I should be thanking you," Lord responded. "He was a thorn in both of our sides. Now he's finally out of our hair and we can make that money."

"I'm gonna need another favor real soon," I said.

"Well, so far you're batting a hundred! I feed you info and you take the competition out of their misery. I like that! I guess I was wrong about you, huh?"

"I guess so. But, quite honestly, you haven't seen anything yet!"

151

Back at Innocent's house, I was informed by Crystal that I received two calls all within the last hour: one from the "lettermen" – Special Agents Johnson and Samuels, and the other from Lincoln.

"Why the f**k is Lincoln and those FBI clowns calling me at the house?" I said to no one in particular.

Before Crystal had a chance to respond, another call came in. This time it was a collect call from my brother.

"Those FBI dudes are sweatin' me," I told him.

"I know. Word on the street is they're lookin' to use you to help them get the drop on Spanky and the rest of his crew."

"I'm no snitch. I'll get Spanky myself."

"Who you think you are? The Godfather or something? I don't need you up in here with me. There's too much money to be made out there. If something happens to you, the family business comes to an end. Understand me?"

"Stimey paid me a visit at Pop's funeral."

"Did he? Watch your back with him. He rolls deep."

"So do I, bro! So do I!"

My brother and I often used names off of old television shows in case the phones were bugged. For that previous conversation, we did our best rendition of *The Little Rascals*. "Spanky" referred to Lincoln, and "Stimey" referred to Trevor. It was a ploy that had always worked to our advantage. I then updated him on my "discovery" at Pop's house and the letters that were in his glove compartment.

"I got some more news for you, lil' brother."

"What?"

"It's about your boy Tone."

"I haven't heard from him in a minute. I cut him loose."

"Well, some of my people in here informed me that he's now running with Trevor! And he's a straight user! Stays coked up every minute of the day. Can't get enough of that white stuff."

"If he's sleeping with the enemy, then he will get it, as well.

Good lookin' out."

My conversation with Innocent was prematurely halted by a phone check from one of the C.O.'s, just as T.J. was eagerly waiting to hear his father's voice. Crystal didn't think I knew, but I recently overheard her on the phone with a potential love interest. Couldn't say I blamed her. Innocent was in jail for the rest of his life. That didn't mean her life had to end...and Innocent wouldn't hear the news from me.

It was time to get a good night's rest. Tomorrow we would all meet up at a new destination chosen by Lincoln to drop off his monthly "hush money". Afterwards, we were going to have to come to blows with Trevor and possibly his new foot soldier, Tone. The plot thickens!

CHAPTER THIRTEEN

For all the drugs I had ever seen, I never sold directly to anyone or used the stuff. Not even marijuana. Everyone in the crew had jokes about me for not smoking the stuff. All the stories about basehead women prostituting their children and crackhead fiends stealing to support their habit had always been a major turnoff, and as far as I was concerned, drugs was drugs. No such thing as a "harmless" drug. Innocent had suggested that I visit one of the crack houses that we maintained out in East Flatbush in order to keep myself grounded. According to his and my pop's theory, if I made it an annual ritual, I would never be tempted to try the stuff. Not that I had any plans to do so anyway. I was accompanied by Swift. Drac was taking care of other important matters and couldn't make the trip.

"Yo, this place is off the hook!" Swift said, lighting up a marijuana-filled blunt.

"What did I tell you about smoking that s**t in my ride! I swear if we get pulled over…"

"You worry too much. Between the air freshener and gum, you can't even smell anything. Besides, I need to get a little weeded up before walking up in there. That house is depressing as all hell!"

"When was the last time you visited the house?"

"It's been a minute. Maybe like two, three months. The last time we had to make a trip out here, I got Tone to do it for me. I couldn't stomach seeing all them lost souls up in there."

To hear Swift talk like that really had me on edge because nothing ever bothered him. Or at least that was the image he consistently portrayed in front of everyone. Out of everyone in the crew, he would be the one I would expect to not give a f**k about a pregnant basehead or crack fiend offering their body for a quick fix.

"Make this turn right here," Swift said. "There's the house right there on the corner."

I had over seven crack houses that were maintained by several runners throughout Brooklyn, but I had always made it a point not to visit, until today. The crack house looked anything like what I depicted. However, I still expected the worse as I walked up the steps and entered through the front door. As expected, it was a scene straight out of *New Jack City*. Three young girls dressed very provocatively were coming down the stairs, and three male figures were walking down behind them. One of the men was still fixing his pants zipper, which was a clear indicator of what just transpired.

"Who are y'all?" I said to the three male individuals.

"We came to collect on what was owed to us," one of them responded.

"You got any blow?" one of the girls asked. She then proceeded to walk closer to me, and before I could move away, she took her hands and began unzipping my zipper.

"Get the f**k off of me!" I yelled.

I had my gun drawn, as did Swift, who recently had been allowed to start carrying as long as he promised to follow the art of subtlety, especially when provoked. Now was not one of those times. The three men quickly scurried out the front door and made their way to their car which was parked behind the house.

"I own this house," I said to the three fiends. "Go on and get out of here."

"What did you do that for?" Swift questioned. "They earned their right to stay here and get high. Leave them be."

In another room of the house, I was taken aback by the sight of a crack fiend who was busy milking her visibly-premature infant. In one hand, she was holding a baby bottle, and immediately in front of her on a table were a pipe and some white substance that appeared to be obvious remnants of crack cocaine. I had seen enough and was ready to depart. For once, Swift was in agreement.

"I guess you won't be back to any of the houses anytime soon, huh?" Swift said jokingly.

"Hell no! I just visited my last crack house and I'm never going back. That's why I got you to do my dirty work for me!"

I had been extra cautious about my lettermen visitors since Special Agents Johnson and Samuels made their initial visit. So, I called everyone to meet up at Swift's apartment instead of the usual location.

"Change of plans, y'all," I said. "We're not making a move on Lincoln. Not yet anyway."

"I'm kind of glad, but why not?" Swift questioned.

"'Cause Innocent shut it down. We go after Lincoln, and we will have the entire Brooklyn police force after us. Besides, I think I know how to put the fix on Lincoln, and without gunfire."

"What's your plan?" Drac questioned.

"I'll fill everyone in with the details in due time. Just have faith in ya boy!"

Also present were Jackie, Marley, and Fredro. Without Tone's presence, my two young guns were now that much more valuable to me. They both reacted on cue and had a soldier's mentality: follow orders without asking questions, which was a perfect combination. I felt like a general with my troops sitting around a round table, absorbing my every word like it was the gospel of the Lord. Gone were the days in which bullets were sprayed across three lanes of traffic to get to the opposing force. In my crew, camouflage and subtlety was the key. Enter Jackie.

"You hook up anything with Trevor yet?" I asked.

Jackie nodded her head.

"That's good. I'm going to need you to get him open and vulnerable, but quickly. By now, he knows about Preemo, and he's gonna be looking to retaliate. I know him, and I know his way of thinking. He's not gonna let us think we got one over on him."

I informed everyone of my visits from the lettermen, my trip to Crime's house and the journal, as well as my conversation with Innocent.

"There's another matter we need to deal with," Swift blurted out.

"What's that?" I responded.

"Tone. He's been runnin' his mouth in the streets. He's talking real reckless about getting back at you for what you did to him that day in your brother's backyard."

"Tell him to bring it! From what I hear, he ain't nothin' but a coke fiend looking for his next hit!"

"Those are the ones you have to worry about the most," Drac interrupted.

Before we all separated, everyone had their tasks to handle. Drac headed back to my brother's house to look after Crystal and little T.J. The way things were looking, they were going to need it. Marley and Fredro's job was to shut Tone's mouth. They knew where he hung out at, and more importantly, they were young and fearless. The kind of soldiers to walk right up to Tone and take him out without remorse or hesitation. Swift's job was to close a deal for me out in Canarsie. For about a month now, I had been setting up a business transaction with a couple of Latinos that were known for their high-grade quality marijuana. They always had clientele and remained under the radar of law enforcement. My most important task I left for Jackie. Even at that moment, she was busy texting Trevor and making arrangements for later so he could meet up with her at the strip club where she worked.

"Tell him to come through with two of his boys for Marisol and Yvonne," I said.

Jackie nodded her head in agreement before heading out the front door.

And my job? I kept that from the rest of the crew. I was headed over to Angel's apartment to try and work out our fading relationship. With a baby soon due, there was no way I was going to start things off by being a part-time father. She may have been creeping around on me, but I will be damned if I doom myself to eighteen straight years of paying child support!

I arrived at Angel's apartment in record time to the sound of tears and unfamiliar voices coming from inside her apartment.

"What the hell is going on now?" I said to myself.

I got greeted with looks of disdain and apathy from Angel's on again, off again roommate, Katrina. Also present were two uniformed officers that appeared to be taking down notes.

"You did this!" she blurted out, catching me totally off guard.

"Did what? What the hell are you talking about?"

"Angel is missing, Prentice! Don't act like you don't know what happened!"

Both officers got in between the two of us, as Katrina looked like she was about to start swinging on me.

"Who says she's missing? She's probably over her mother's house. Or better yet, the clown she's sleeping with! Yeah, I know all about that!"

"She stopped dealing with Dayvon after you threatened his life. Or are you going to deny that, as well?"

I didn't respond to Katrina's ranting and raving for fear of incriminating myself in front of the officers. I was escorted into Angel's kitchen for questioning by one of the officers, and I gave my honest account on the situation at hand. Meanwhile, in the other room, I could hear Katrina telling the officer about my "extracurricular activities" and what I did for a living.

Is there any truth to my alleged dealings of illegal drugs? Could this be retaliation to my knowledge of finding out about Angel's affairs? Do I have a history of domestic abuse? When was the last time Angel and I were together?

Those were just some of the questions asked by the officer who was now taking notes and recording them onto a small notepad. But, I had questions of my own.

How long had Angel been missing? Has her mother been contacted? Has anyone contacted Dayvon, the guy she had been sleeping around with?

By the time the two officers compiled their information, I knew the overall basics of the investigation: A frantic message was left for Katrina on the apartment answering machine by Angel. She stated a car pulled up to her as she was getting ready to walk into her apartment, and then her frantic message stopped in mid-conversation. Dayvon was contacted, and he swore he had not seen or heard from Angel since he called to inform her that I had paid him a visit. Also notified was her mother, who has not seen her in several days, and her employer that reported that she was present at work and left for the day an hour before the message was left.

All in all, I was left face to face with a teary-eyed woman who was still giving me her signature look of disdain and apathy.

"Who did this?" she questioned, now slightly calmer than before.

"I don't know, but I will make them pay!"

"You think she was kidnapped?"

The thought did cross my mind while entering the apartment, and hearing myself admit to it only left me that much more looking forward to retaliation.

"I think she was. I KNOW she was!"

"What are we going to do to get her back, Prentice?"

Then it hit me. I was defenseless. While the cops did their preliminary investigation, all I could do was wait for a phone call.

Juice and respect meant everything. Whoever said otherwise said that because they didn't have any. Undoubtedly, they were the two most important character traits to convey when you were in the business I was in.

A mid-afternoon collect phone call from Innocent informed me of who was coming home today: "Extra Black" or E-Black for short. He got his nickname for obvious reasons; he made Wesley Snipes look like an albino! He was also a power player in the drug game before he got put away for armed robbery along with several other charges that were trumped up, but stuck with him nonetheless. He would have gotten away if the getaway driver didn't get a flat tire and drive into a nearby lake, right after hitting a woman on a bike. It also didn't help that the woman was working as an intern for the mayor of New York City! The sentence for his crime: fifteen years of federal time. On that day, he was being released, and Innocent asked me to pick him up. An honor considering the work him and my brother used to put in back in the day before I was barely allowed to cross the street on my old block.

"You've been real quiet the entire ride here. What's up with you?" Swift questioned.

"Nothing. I'm good."

"Nothing my a**! Something's up. What's good?"

"Man, I just found out Angel's missing. I think she was kidnapped."

"Damn, man. When did you find this out?"

"Last night. I can't do anything until I get a phone call of some kind."

"Don't worry, man. Everything will work itself out."

There was an uncomfortable silence as we waited for E-Black to make his arrival. Swift was looking through my iPod selection, trying his best to avoid saying anything that may remind me of what recently transpired with Angel.

"You think something happened to E-Black?" Swift asked. "He was one crazy dude back in the day. You and I were just shorties when he ran things. You think he'll remember us?"

"I know he'll remember me. He better! He probably just got caught up with some legal paperwork or something. He should be coming out soon."

E-Black was fierce in his heyday, truly a man amongst boys. Sure enough, a wide-shouldered figure with a knapsack over his back was walking towards my ride. It was a familiar face that belonged to none other than the infamous E-Black, a street hustler slash hitman that once made Innocent look like a boy scout in training.

"Yo, E, what's good? Welcome home!" I exclaimed.

"Peace, my young brother," E-Black responded. "But, I don't go by that name anymore. E-Black was my name when I was runnin' around aimlessly in the streets. I'm a new man. My mind has been reborn."

"Stop playin', E!" Swift added. "You must not remember who you're talking to. Seriously though, I know you can't wait to get back out here and do your thing, right? Take back what's yours."

"No, young brother, I'm serious. I left that life just like I just left out of that prison behind us. There is only one of two places to end up. Either where I just walked out of or buried six feet under."

Damn! That was all I needed. The one man that could have solidified my status in the streets was now just a shell of his former self. If I had known that, I would've kept my Black a** home! Unless, of course, he was testing us to see what we were really about, and he was really looking forward to reclaiming his name in the streets. Nonetheless, it was refreshing to see a face from back in the day that was an icon in the streets. Just the fact that E-Black was home should make a few heads run for the hills.

After dropping off the man formerly known as E-Black at his son's mother's house, I returned to my own domicile to await further information about Angel. As instructed, both Marley and Fredro were waiting for me to pull up to the curb.

"So did y'all take care of that?" I questioned, referring to catching up with Tone and making an example out him for some of his alleged trash-mouth talking.

"He was rollin' with a crew of people when we saw him. Like six or seven of them were all walking down Church Avenue. It didn't make any sense steppin' to him like that," Fredro said.

"I want to catch him alone. Swift, you gotta know where he stays at. What about his people? The two of you go back how many years?" I asked.

"He hasn't been at his old place in a minute now. He moved out and has been living over in Farragut Projects from what I heard. I have no idea where his people stay at, or if he even has any people left living in New York."

"Say no more," Marley interrupted. "We're on it. I got some people out in Farragut Projects. I'll look into it."

Both Marley and Fredro rode off on their bikes, most likely towards the same projects Tone was now staying at.

"What are you going to do about Angel?" Swift questioned.

"We need to get the word out that anyone who knows anything about what went down will be dealt with!"

"Man, I don't even know. But, I can't just sit here doing nothing."

Swift departed, leaving me by myself for some much-needed time to contemplate what was going on in Innocent's house for probably the first time ever. Leaving me with the time I needed to reevaluate my life's choices.

"I only have one choice," I said to myself, while searching one of my previously worn pair of pants for the lettermen's phone number.

CHAPTER FOURTEEN

One more trip out to West Virginia was what I needed to get my mind right and my pockets a little fatter. A last minute call from my country connects Wild Bob and Bear put me on to a very lucrative offer. It was enough money that I could leave this life of looking over my shoulder and going to bed wondering if I was going to see the next day. With a son or a daughter on the way, it was definitely not the way I wanted to live my life or raise a child. I accepted their invite and immediately began making plans to take the ten-hour drive by myself.

At a local bodega, my intention was to grab some snacks and a couple of Red Bull energy drinks for the ride, but I was called out by an old acquaintance. It was Felix, the speedy Hispanic dude from my football team.

"I heard you're the man now," he said excitedly. "The man who's still walking around with that geeky book bag across his back! Put me down so I can handle my business. Money's real tight out here, and I got bills and a little one to look after."

"Shhh! Keep your voice down. Come on, let's go outside and talk."

David L.

I warned him of the obvious dangers that came with my line of work, but he was persistent. He appeared desperate and continued to remind me of his three-year-old daughter and baby mama that kept giving him grief about the lack of money he was bringing into the apartment.

"See me when I get back. I might have some work for you," I promised.

I had never seen Felix as the type of individual that could push weight or hold down a block, but six months ago, anyone could've said the same thing about me.

After filling up with gas in New Jersey, I stopped by my brother's old gun connect in Paterson where they did more than just sell guns.

"I need you to hook up my ride," I said.

In other words, I needed some work done in order to conceal the thirty thousand dollars in cash and coke that I was keeping in a book bag hidden in the trunk of my car, which was also the first place the boys in blue would check if I happened to get pulled over.

"So what kind of gun do you need?" Dillinger, the boss man of the entire operation, questioned. "Your brother is good people and always had my money on time. I will give you the same deal I used to give him."

"No guns for me. Not today anyway. I need you to do something with my ride. I'm on my way to West Virginia."

After explaining what needed to be done, Dillinger put one of his best men on the job. About an hour and a half later, my prized Dodge Charger was ready to hit the road. I now had hidden compartments in the spare tire in the trunk, taillights, headlights, and dashboard of my ride. The entire operation cost a little over two thousand dollars, which was a small cost to pay for my freedom if I happened to get pulled over. After Dillinger finished concealing the cash and the drugs, a bloodhound couldn't detect anything in my ride.

"My condolences regarding your brother," Dillinger said to

166

me as I got ready to depart. "Give him my blessings."

"I'll tell him you hooked me up. He will appreciate it."

Dillinger was one of those rare individuals that exuded professionalism. A man of his word, and more importantly, he always did good work. At least that was what Innocent used to tell me. I handed him another three hundred dollars as a tip for the great job on my ride and promised to send more business his way.

West Virginia. Similar to my previous visit, I was again treated with warmth and care, while my every need and want was granted by the same two individuals I came to meet with that day: a couple of slick-talking White boys who, from the time I had met them, treated me probably better than over ninety percent of the individuals that inhabited my hood. I was greeted at the city line welcoming station by Wild Bob and Bear, then immediately brought to a crowded restaurant to conduct business. On arrival, I was one of only a few people of color in the establishment. However, I was treated as if the color of my skin was insignificant. After all, the color of my money was what everyone was interested in!

"I see you're still traveling with that kiddy book bag!" Wild Bob said jokingly.

"I keep it with me wherever I go. I don't look as intimidating to cops when I carry it with me. It makes me look studious."

"Well, has it worked?"

"Nope. Not a bit!"

"You're gonna either end up dead or in jail like your brother," Bear said matter-of-factly and totally out of the blue. He was keeping himself busy by meticulously rolling up some chewing tobacco and feeling in his pockets for matches. "We don't touch the stuff. But, you – you're right smack in the middle of it all. Right now, you can be touched. Hell, the cops are probably on to you more than anyone else in the hood!"

"So what do you suggest?" I responded. "You rather I send someone else to do these types of big money drop offs? With your money? Your coke? And then what? They leave town with my loot and my drugs…never to be heard from again?"

"We do what we do because our money is long. We are what you would call untouchable. You're not. Every Tom, Dick, and Harry is ready and willing to gun you down and take over your small-scale operation, including those you think are loyal to you."

In the midst of thinking over what Bear had just said to me, I slid under the table thirty thousand in cash, as well as another fifteen thousand of the best cocaine I could get my hands on with such short notice. Neither of them even considered counting it. That's how much I was respected. Either that or my brother's name still rang bells all the way out there in the middle of nowhere.

"So what's this big thing that's supposed to change my life?" I asked.

A couple more locals entered the establishment and made themselves comfortable at one of the many tables that surrounded the restaurant. Almost everyone that entered made it a point to acknowledge Wild Bob and Bear with a head nod or walk over and shake their hands.

"You're looking at it," Bear responded.

The confused look on my face prompted Bear to elaborate.

"I can see you require further explanation. Look around you."

"What?"

"It's three o'clock in the darn afternoon! Three f**king o'clock! And this place is already packed to capacity. This place is a goldmine!"

"What does that have to do with anything? You want me to quit what I'm doing and get into the restaurant business?"

"I got two more just like this. They're both in the hood, and I think your slick, smooth, New York savvy style is the perfect piece of the puzzle. What'cha say?"

I was momentarily left alone to marinate in my thoughts. Looking around, the place was a goldmine. Three o'clock on a Tuesday afternoon no less! But West Virginia? I had been contemplating a career readjustment, but too much was going on right now. Angel was missing. I had a child on the way. And my family needed me. Little T.J. needed me.

"Give me some time to think it over," I told Bear, who returned with a couple of well-endowed waitresses in an obvious attempt to help sway my thought process.

"Okay. Think it over, but don't take too long. This offer we're giving you isn't going to last forever."

I had a lot to contemplate, but the good thing was I had a ten-hour drive back to Brooklyn, which would be more than enough time to give their job opportunity some serious consideration.

My return to Brooklyn was not without the ongoing controversy that made up my life. I received a text message from Katrina, Angel's roommate, pleading for me to come over to the house as soon as possible. I obliged without question. Sensing a possible problem, I immediately notified the troops to meet me there. Both Drac and Swift arrived moments after I got there.

"What's wrong?" I asked.

"Read this," Katrina responded.

I read the typewritten note privately and then out loud for

David L.

the others to hear.

You didn't want to do things my way, so I had no choice but to up the ante. In other words, you got too big for your own good. My question to you, Prentice Barnes, is this: Is your girl and your unborn child worth $50,000? That's how much it's going to cost if you ever want to see your girl again. Check your car's windshield right now for part two of this note.

I motioned for Swift to retrieve the other half of the note for me to read. Sure enough, it was posted on my windshield, which meant I was probably followed there and the perpetrator knew my every move. I quickly opened the envelope and continued reading for everyone to hear.

Bring the money tomorrow at six p.m. to the same diner you decided not to pay me my money. There's going to be a black Mercedes Benz parked behind the diner. The doors will be unlocked. You are to open the back door and place the money in the back seat. Put the money in a garbage bag. If you try anything funny or bring the police with you, I will personally perform my own special abortion on your girl. Then I'm going to kill her, take pictures, and drop the pictures off to your brother's front doorstep. Challenge me if you think I'm bluffing.

Everyone in the apartment was speechless, including me. They were waiting to see how I responded. Well, everyone except Katrina.

"Goddamn, Prentice! This is your entire fault! You and your drug-pushing friends standing here! Now what are you going to do?"

Swift attempted to add his two cents, but he was immediately ordered to fall back and silence himself.

"Calm down, Katrina. I'm going to fix everything. I'll get her back. Relax and keep your mouth shut. Don't notify the police AND don't leave the apartment for any reason whatsoever! They may come looking for you next."

With nothing more that could be accomplished there, Drac, Swift, and I headed back to Innocent's house to devise a

170

counterattack. Before doing so, I immediately called Tammy and alerted her of what just happened and ordered her to remain indoors.

"You know this has Lincoln written all over it, right?" Swift said.

"I know it does."

"So what are you gonna do? You pay him that ransom money and there's no guarantee he's gonna even release Angel."

"I know that, too. But, I think I know a couple of guys that want Lincoln as much as I do."

"Who?"

"Patience. I'll explain everything when the time is right."

The next day, I got ready to head to my destination fifteen minutes early. I couldn't take any chances of getting caught up in traffic.

"We should go with you," Drac said.

Also present was Marley and Fredro, who were both picked up the previous day by undercover for suspicious activities while hanging out on their block. However, they were released shortly afterwards for lack of any incriminating evidence.

"This is something I have to do myself," I responded.

"Well then, at least take this," Swift said, handing me a nickel-plated pistol.

"I'm not going there strapped. Lincoln is probably going to have a bunch of his boys in blue tailing him. If I get pulled over with that piece on me, I'm a goner. I can't take that chance."

"I still don't agree with any of this. You need your boys in a time like this."

"Just listen out for my call...and go over to my sister's house and check up on her. You can help me by doing that for me."

There was no black Mercedes in sight as I pulled up behind the diner. I could feel my heart racing from the anticipation building up within me. As instructed, I had fifty thousand dollars in cash in a garbage bag, and according to the note, I should be expecting my company shortly. Over thirty cars had driven past me, none of which was a black Mercedes.

"What if this is all a ploy and no one is coming here today?" I said to myself.

As my mind continued to create various scenarios, my cell phone rang.

"Who is it?" I answered anxiously.

"It's me...Katrina."

"What's the matter? I'm kind of busy right now."

"I received another note that someone slid under my front door. It says to leave the money in the red BMW parked across from you with the President Obama bumper sticker."

"Of course! Something told me I was going to be double-crossed."

"Why do you say that? There's no BMW where you're at?"

"No, there's one. It's been parked here at the diner since I got here several minutes ago. But now, I have no idea who is behind the kidnapping. I was hoping to confront the perpetrator. Or at least get a glimpse of what he looked like. I have an idea who it is, but there's no way I would be able to prove it now."

I ended my conversation with Katrina and made my move over to the parked BMW. I tried my best to look indiscreet, but that was a tall order for a Black man in the middle of the day walking over to another vehicle with a three-ply garbage bag full of money carried over his shoulder. As expected, the back door of the BMW was left unlocked for me, so I quickly placed the bag onto the seat, where a note was left in plain view for my reading pleasure.

If you're reading this, then you obviously know how to follow instructions. I have one more job for you. After you do this last job for me, your girl will be returned to you. Look under the front seat. There's an address written on a piece of paper. You will find Lincoln there in his car parked outside at approximately ten p.m. next Sunday night. Kill him and your precious Angel will be returned to you within the hour. Don't kill Lincoln or try to double-cross me by bringing the cops, and you will never see her again. Seven days.

Once again, my head was racing with thoughts and questions left unanswered. So if Lincoln didn't kidnap Angel, then who? Do I have a traitor in my crew? Drac? Swift? All I knew was I was way over my head, and I was going to need as much help as possible to get out of it. This was one situation all of the money, power, and respect in the world were not going to get me out of.

CHAPTER FIFTEEN

Marley and Fredro were on Pitkin Avenue waiting for me to arrive. A few side jobs here and there, and I would be able to recoup the fifty thousand I paid Angel's abductor in no time. Although wet behind the ears in age, both of my young guns continued to do what they knew best, which was sell those rocks to fiends throughout the neighborhood. Before I even pulled up to the apartment building they were hustling out of, they had already grossed a little over a grand in less than thirty minutes of work. I was greeted with the utmost respect upon my arrival, complements of the notoriety from Innocent and his continued presence in the streets that I dwelled in.

"What up, P?" one hustler yelled out as I pulled up to the curb. "We don't see you out here in these parts too often. It's an honor."

I smiled to myself, not because of my homegrown legendary status, but because Marley and Fredro had runners working for them more than twice their age! Presently, everyone was happy because they were eating in the streets, but don't get it twisted. The moment money began to dry up, my rep would be on the line – and possibly my safety. That was why I continued to pay everyone top dollar. To keep them satisfied, but not so satisfied that they no longer required my supervision and protection.

"Where is this new cat you wanted to introduce us to?" Marley questioned.

"Give him a few minutes. He'll be here," I replied.

I watched in dismay as the seconds ticked away on my newly-purchased Rolex watch. Not because I was waiting for someone to arrive to introduce Marley and Fredro to, but because every second that escaped me meant less time to figure out a way to save my girl and unborn child. I had been privately coming up with baby names for my little one, and the thought alone almost brought me to tears. Fredro got my attention during my momentary lapse in concentration. I had come to grips with what had transpired, and there was a very good chance that Angel would never be returned to me. Not alive anyway.

"Is that him?"

"Yeah, that's him."

My old football partner Felix walked over to the three of us and introduced himself to Fredro and Marley.

"Take care of my boy here," I said to both of them. "Start him off slow, but keep him in the loop. Watch his back, but also let him stand on his own."

"He's good here with us," Fredro responded. "There's plenty of money to be made here. Just don't get greedy and think you can sell to everyone that comes over to you."

The operation was simple, yet almost foolproof. The workday began at nine a.m. sharp. Why so early? Because fiends don't sleep, and once the sun comes up, they want to get that next hit. A sale was only made when the fiend showed their cash that was attached to a red money clip. No red money clip meant no sale. There was a lookout person set up on both sides of the block. Another runner was always seated in a black Nissan Sentra parked immediately across the street in case one time made themselves known.

"I've been getting money from this spot for over four months now, so if this block gets hot, I'm personally blaming it on you," I warned, looking directly at Felix.

"Don't sell no product to anyone unless the money is accompanied by a red money clip…no matter what they tell you. Got it?"

"I got it."

"Good. Make sure you call me later. We'll talk and you can let me know how your first day went. Oh yeah, and one more thing…"

"What's that?"

"We can't call you by your government no longer. That ain't gonna work. On the block your new name is Flash."

"Flash?"

"Yeah 'cause you was always one fast a** mutha******!"

I had six days left. A phone call from Innocent to get some much-needed advice proved unsuccessful due to him getting into a verbal altercation with one of the prison guards and ending up again in the hole. So, I was left alone to figure things out for myself. If Pops were still alive, him and I would've brainstormed together and came up with a way to get me out of the mess I was in. With nothing to do but wait out the next six days, I decided to pay my only other close family member alive a visit – my sister Tammy.

"What should I do?" I asked, referring to my awkward predicament.

"I'm no genius, Prentice, but it smells like a set-up."

"How so?"

"You go there to that location waving your guns in the air

and looking for that dirty cop, and you're going to be sharing a cell with Innocent. I say don't even go."

"Are you serious? Don't go! I know you never liked Angel, but damn! She's carrying my son...or daughter. Your nephew or niece."

"I'm sorry. You came here looking for advice, right? What do you want me to tell you? To go there and get yourself killed? I just buried my father. I'm not going to another funeral until it is time! You hear me, Prentice?"

Before I had a chance to respond, the text I had been waiting for had arrived: Trevor is picking me up in one hour. Going back to my place for drinks.

Never too big on texting, I decided to follow-up with Jackie with a phone call instead.

"Give me your address so I can add it to my GPS," I said.

"Will do. I'm in the first-floor apartment."

"Are you crazy or something? Why is he coming to your apartment?"

"I'm actually sub-leasing it through one of the bouncers from the club. I can't be traced to it."

"Good. Good. Leave the front door unlocked for me. Text me when I got the green light to enter."

"I will. I have some pills that will put him out like a baby."

"Damn, girl! You think of everything. Where did you get them from?"

"Come on now, P. A girl can't reveal all of her tricks."

"Well don't kill the man! I need him alive to answer some questions. Just touch up his drink enough so that I can move in on him without any resistance."

"I got you. I will text you when it's time."

"Okay. I'm going to call the crew now, and I'll see you in a little bit."

For once in a very long time, I had received some good news. Trevor had to be involved with everything that was going on. The letter from my pops confirmed he was bitter about not being brought up in the ranks to take over. Trevor looked at me as a reminder to what he could've had…similar to someone jilted at the altar and then that person turns around and is married within thirty days. For once, good news, and I was going to savor it while I could.

Location: 177 Clinton Avenue. I had gotten to my destination along with Swift and Drac in less than fifteen minutes. According to the text I received from Jackie a few moments ago, the drug she slipped Trevor should've been taking effect right at that moment. The building Jackie inhabited seemed very familiar to the abandoned building I met up with Lord and Wise in. Somehow, I was always under the impression that Jackie was much too upscale to reside at a place similar to the one I was walking into.

"It's about to be on!" Swift said excitedly.

"Exactly what do you want to do?" Drac asked.

"Answers…I want answers. If he's a traitor and all signs point to him that he is, then he will be dealt with."

"You never did tell us the address to where Angel's abductor wants you to take out Lincoln," Swift said.

"Where the aquarium is located over in Coney Island."

"You think it's a set-up?"

"I'm sure it is."

No one else appeared to inhabit the building, so noise wouldn't be a factor. The three of us were positioned immediately outside the front door, waiting to get the next text from Jackie. Unable to wait any longer, I sent her a text of my own, asking if we had the green light to enter. We did. Swift turned the doorknob ever so slightly, and we entered Jackie's apartment with our guns drawn and guards up.

"They're in the back room," Swift whispered. "I can hear their voices and see their reflection from the television."

"Keep your safety on, and don't even think about firing," I responded, looking directly at Swift.

We were now standing immediately behind the bedroom door. Jackie saw us from the corner of her eye as she was ejecting a disc out of the DVD player and making meaningless conversation to keep Trevor preoccupied until we could make our move. Trevor was sitting up on the bed and totally oblivious to the three of us standing behind him.

"Turn your b***h a** around!" I said, while aiming my piece in his direction.

He turned around as requested with only a hint of surprise. I was almost disappointed that I didn't get the reaction I was so looking forward to.

"Yo, he must really be f**ked up," Swift commented.

He appeared to be only semi-conscious, complements of the drugs Jackie slipped into his drink earlier.

"I don't think you're gonna get much outta him right now," Jackie said. "You may wanna try him again in the morning so you can get him out of here."

Jackie was correct. Not about removing him from her apartment, but the fact that he was not in any condition to do any meaningful talking. Besides, I had waited this long. What were a few more hours anyway in the grand scheme of things? I sent Swift to get the rope from my ride to tie up Trevor until we returned the following morning.

"This should hold him for the night," I said, doing my best boy scout impersonation with my knots.

"Don't cut off his circulation!" Jackie responded. "Gag up his mouth for me, too. I don't want to have to hear him pleading for me to untie him in the middle of the night. The stuff I slipped into his drink will probably wear off in a few hours."

"Good," I replied. "We'll be back for him when the sun comes up. Get yourself a good night's rest until we return."

It was only poetic justice that I told Jackie to get a good night's rest but couldn't get one myself. I was still suffering from the same nightmares I started having right after Preemo was murdered. There must have been a connection. Or maybe that was my subconscious telling me that I wasn't built for what I was doing. No matter. Soon enough, I would be closer to vindication.

As promised, we returned to Jackie's apartment just as the morning sun had ascended to its highest point in the sky. It was a beautiful morning, and it was about to be made even more captivating by who I had inside waiting for me. Inside Jackie's apartment, her two partners in crime, Marisol and Yvonne, were also present.

"What are y'all doing here?" I questioned.

"Mrs. Scaredy Cat didn't want to be here by herself," Yvonne responded. "She's in the back waiting for you."

"All that tough talk and you would think she could handle a man tied up in her bedroom," I responded.

Sure enough, Trevor was fully awake, trying desperately to unloosen himself from the rope I tied around him several hours previously. I did him one better: I took the gag from out of his mouth.

"What the f**k is this about, Prentice?" Trevor yelled out. "F**king untie me right now!"

"You ain't in any condition to be making demands," I responded. "Matter of fact, keep talkin' s**t and I'll put the gag back in your mouth!"

Trevor called my bluff by continuing to rant and rave until a well-placed slap to his face momentarily reminded him of who was in charge.

"Lemme get a piece of him!" Swift requested.

Swift was aptly ignored so I could begin my interrogation. Trevor had hustled in the streets most of his life and been in and out of jail. So, asking him a bunch of questions was not going to do the trick. No, I had to devise a scheme to make him answer my questions willingly. I motioned for Jackie to bring me a hanger from the closet. I proceeded to bend the hanger back and then sent Swift into the kitchen to place it under a flame for about a minute.

"What are you going to do with that?" Trevor questioned.

"I'm not going to do anything with it if you tell me everything I need to know," I replied.

"Like what? I don't know what the f**k you're talking about!"

"You were working with Preemo, right? You and him had plans on taking me out?"

"Me and him had some side jobs together. So what? But then he got taken out, so I figured that was my chance to step up and make some power moves. You taking him out actually helped me out. How could I get mad at that?"

"What about Tone?"

"What about him? He put the word out that he wanted to do some runs for me. I was suspicious at first with everything that was going down, but he checked out."

"And the million-dollar question...Lincoln?"

"He and I had an altercation a few weeks ago. I don't do business with him any longer. Whatever is going down between the two of you, I have nothing to do with."

I grabbed the hanger from Swift and placed it closer to Trevor's forehead.

"Don't f**king lie to me! My girl was kidnapped. You may not have done it, but you know something!"

"I don't know what you're talking about! I had nothing to do with your girl being kidnapped!"

"Wrong answer!"

The searing heat from the tip of the hanger touched Trevor's forehead ever so slightly, enough to make him scream out in agony.

"I swear I don't know anything about that!" Trevor repeated.

"I have five days to figure out what happened to my girl, and I know somehow you're involved."

"What makes you think I have anything to do with that?"

"I'm tired of his stalling," Swift interrupted, grabbing the hanger out of my hand.

"I'm going to reheat this, and when I get back, I'm gonna carve my initials into your skull."

"Yo, P, don't do this," Trevor begged. "I don't deserve this!"

"You sold my family out when my father didn't give you the second-in-command title. You helped set my brother up, and in the process, got him locked away for life. I know all about the conversation you and my pops had when y'all met up in the Bronx back in March and he turned down your request to be his lieutenant. And don't think I forgot about what happened with Trip. I almost caught a bullet over that one!"

"Trip and I never got along. He and I always had our little differences, but I didn't kill him, if that's what you mean."

"You're a lying son of a b***h!"

Swift returned with the hanger and the tip was now a crimson red. Even Jackie, as hardcore as she could be at times, turned her head to avoid seeing what may have happened next if I didn't get the information I was looking for.

"I'm gonna give you one more chance to talk!" I said.

However, my attempts proved to be futile. Either Trevor could withstand inhuman amounts of torture, or he really didn't know anything. Either way, I instinctively knew I couldn't allow him to go free. I also knew he was the one that placed a bounty on my head, so taking him out would not be a problem for me.

"Swift, suffocate his punk a**! Then come back tonight

when it's dark and take the body someplace where it won't be found."

"With pleasure! It's about time you let me do something!"

CHAPTER SIXTEEN

With Trevor dead and finally out of my life forever, my realization of a drug monopoly was beginning to see some life, except I no longer wanted to live that way and a relocation to West Virginia was becoming more and more attractive. Angel's kidnapping, the many deaths I had witnessed and was responsible for in those last several months, and all the deception and betrayal was starting to take a toll on my sanity. Betrayal being the emphasis.

"Hurry up and get down here, P," Swift said through his cell phone. "We got problems out here on Marley and Fredro's post."

"What kind of problems?" I questioned. "These are things I would expect you to handle as my second-in-command."

"Problems I don't want to get into over the phone. How soon before you can get down here?"

"Give me about half an hour, but I'm telling you, Swift…this better be important or else!"

Upon my arrival, everyone present wanted to talk all at once. Pedestrians were standing around as if there was something to see. That's when it hit me that something must

David L.

have recently happened. That would be the only explanation for the random stares that came from across the street...and down the block.

"This better be good for you to get me out of my bed," I said to Swift.

Around him were several low-level drug runners and lookout men whose names I couldn't remember, but who ultimately all worked for me. Ominously missing in action were Fredro, Marley, and my newest recruit, Flash.

"Where are the others?" I asked.

"That's what I've been tryin' to tell you," Swift responded. "Marley and Fredro were nabbed by undercover. Picked up right before I called to tell you to get down here. They got busted working the block with your boy."

"So then where is Flash? He was working this block with them."

There was momentary silence until one of Swift's low-level runners stepped up to the plate to respond to my inquiry.

"We think your boy Flash is a mole for the cops."

"Why do you say that?"

"You told him not to sell to anyone without a red money clip, right?"

"Yeah, he knows. I told him myself."

"Well, he didn't, but the undercover that nabbed Fredro and Marley HAD a red money clip! And when they made the bust, it was right after your boy Flash took a break to make a potato chip run to the bodega at the corner. That's a helluva coincidence, don't you think?"

There was that looming thought again – betrayal. Everyone was looking at me to give the go ahead for the next move.

"Shut everything down on this block!" I said with a hint of disgust in my voice. "Swift, find another location. No one is to sell on this block again."

"But..."

"What did I just say? NOBODY!"

186

Swift's entourage dispersed, leaving Swift and I to collect our thoughts.

"I didn't want to say anything in front of the others, but I got a call from Tone earlier today," Swift confessed.

"Oh yeah, and?"

"He's on a mission to bring you down. He's talking a lot of s**t and says he's got the manpower AND the loot to bring you down...with or without Trevor."

"What clse did he say?"

"That's about it. We didn't talk for too long, but I do remember him saying something about getting back at you through the people you love."

"He's gotta be referring to either my sister Tammy or..."

"Little T.J.," Swift interrupted.

"Well, that ain't gonna happen. Drac is fighting an infection from that bullet he took coming back from Jersey, and Fredro and Marley were arrested earlier on drug possession charges. So, they're of no help to me right now. That only leaves you, me, and the girls."

"We're gonna need more than that to go up against Tone and his crazy pack of dope fiends he's been associating with. Those guys kill for fun from what I heard."

"I think there's one more person I can call on to get down with us. It's a long shot, though."

"Who?"

"E-Black."

I had three days left to figure out a plan on how to get Angel back to me safely, and at the same time, avoid the probable ambush that was awaiting me. I had gotten off the phone with my two country connects, Wild Bob and Bear, and had taken

David L.

their very lucrative offer to relocate to West Virginia: ninety thousand dollars a year in base salary to run two of their restaurant locations. True, I could've probably made that in about six months in New York, but down there I was much more likely to live to one day see my twenty-fifth birthday.

I returned to the same place I dropped E-Black off after his release from prison.

"Even if I wanted to get back in the business, I'm not the type to be working for anyone. No offense," he said to me.

"No offense taken. I wouldn't expect anything less," I responded. "My time is up in this game. I'm taking my behind down south where I will be alive to see my child take his or her first steps."

I was invited in to discuss things a little further. That alone told me that E-Black was at least contemplating my previous proposal. Word on the street was he had been struggling to get an honest job and his son's mother was continuing to hound him because he had not yet secured employment. As if that was any surprise. Last I checked, not too many employers were eager to hire an ex-felon without a high school diploma straight out of the joint. I was about to change all of that for E-Black.

"You've been out of the game for over a decade, right?" I said. "I've got a little situation going on with my girl, but as soon as everything is straightened out, I'm out of New York forever. That's my word."

"And let me get this right. You want me to be your replacement?"

"It's a little premature to say that, but I think I can smooth everything out with my brother when the time is right. So what do you say? Are you down or what?"

"I'm gonna need some time to think about it."

E-Black gave me that same look I gave Wild Bob and Bear when I was contemplating their offer. It was that look which said, 'I'm interested; however, I don't want to look too eager, so let me play it cool.'

188

"What is there to think about? You're home and haven't found work yet, right? I'm giving you the opportunity of a lifetime. To take over for me so I can get the hell up outta here! So, again, I ask – are you down or what?"

A simple head nod gave me the answer I was looking for.

Although rusty, E-Black was more than qualified to fill my rookie shoes. Swift may have been a little uneasy about the change when I finally decided to tell him, but he would learn to adapt. He was going to have to. Innocent was another story. Although I told E-Black everything was a go, my brother was going to have a problem with me leaving New York for a life down south. So would Pops if he were still alive. This was supposed to be a family business, and I took it upon myself to bring in an outsider.

A few blocks away from my brother's house, I got an urgent call from none other than Carol, my pop's ex-fiancé in Connecticut.

"Are you in some kind of trouble?" she questioned.

"Not that I know of. Why do you ask?"

"Because a couple of men who says they're from the FBI just paid me a visit. They said for you to give them a call immediately, and that you knew how to reach them."

"Did they say anything else?"

"No. They wanted to come inside and check around the house, but I told them unless they had a warrant, that was not going to happen."

"Okay. Thank you, Carol. I'll take care of everything. Don't you worry about nothing."

Less than twenty-four hours later, E-Black got down with me and prepped to be my eventual replacement, and he was already making his presence known in the streets.

"I said strip, mutha******," he said calmly, pointing his nickel-plated pistol toward a local drug runner who had come up fifty dollars short on a final money count. Drac was still home nursing his bullet wound, the girls were all working down at the strip club, and Swift was bent over from laughing so hard at the unfortunate expense of the half-naked man standing across the room from him.

"Take everything off! Down to your s**tty-a** drawers!" E-Black insisted.

And me? What was I doing during that altercation? I was too preoccupied with my thoughts to care. If someone came up short, then they deserved whatever they got. If I didn't learn from my mistakes, then I was doomed to continue making them. I was that same person that E-Black was not too long ago with the way I manhandled and embarrassed Tone. Now, instead of him being an ally to my organization, he had made himself my sworn enemy and was looking to exact revenge on me by any means necessary.

"You never did tell me why we couldn't meet up at your brother's house," Swift said, taking a momentary break from laughing.

"That's not important right now," I responded. "Besides, meeting at Innocent's crib isn't going to go down anymore. Everything is going to go through E's place until further notice."

The real reason for the change was because I had the FBI sniffing up my a**, but Swift or anyone else didn't need to know all of that. Truth be told, the sooner E-Black slid into my position, the faster I could let my family know of my true intentions. Tammy was going to take it the hardest because she had never worked an honest day in her life. Between Pops, Innocent, and now myself, she was always looked after and her bills were always paid for by one of us.

"You better not be short on my money again," E-Black said,

forcing his victim to exit the apartment in only a pair of boxers and socks.

I didn't say anything to him, preferring he follow his own winning brand of authority. Everything E-Black did was usually in excess from what I remembered about him: smoking weed, gambling, spending money recklessly, and drinking. It was only twelve o'clock in the afternoon, and he had already downed five shots of Hennessey. He was an imposing figure, as well, weighing approximately three hundred pounds and standing about six-feet, three-inches tall. He was a modern day Suge Knight.

"Where are you goin'?" Swift questioned, as I grabbed my baseball cap from off the coffee table and made my way towards the door.

"I have a couple of calls to make. One of them is to Lincoln."

"What are you calling him for?"

"My monthly payment."

"I thought you weren't going to pay him any more money."

"I'm not."

"Hey, I got some news that you might find interesting."

"What's that?"

"It's about Tone. This chick I used to mess with out in the projects he stays at told me earlier today that he's out spending money like it's going out of style."

"Yeah? So?"

"You ever think that maybe he has something to do with Angel's abduction? Didn't you recently leave fifty thousand big ones in the back of a parked BMW?"

Once again, I was greeted at the curb by the lettermen,

David L.

Special Agents Johnson and Samuels, as I arrived at my brother's house. Neither of them were dressed like they were on duty, and Johnson was keeping himself preoccupied in the driver's seat by sucking on a fat cigar and blowing rings out of the window.

"You've been a bad boy, Mr. Barnes," Special Agent Samuels said.

"What are you talking about? And watch who you call boy," I responded.

"You're in way over your head, Prentice, and you really should consider letting us help you."

If I decided to involve Johnson and Samuels in my nonsense, I could have jeopardized my entire operation. Worse yet, I would be looked upon as a snitch by everyone that I knew – allies and enemies alike. Where I was from, that was a fate worse than death. Just ask Trevor or Preemo.

"Help me with what? And why are the two of you all over me? I told you before that my brother and I are two completely different people. I don't live that type of lifestyle, so get off of my back!"

I could tell from their facial expressions that neither of them was buying anything I had said.

"That bounty on your head must really be affecting your reasoning," Special Agent Johnson replied sarcastically.

"Exactly what is it that you want from me?" I questioned.

"We want Lincoln, just like you want him. But, you can't get him by yourself…no matter how bad you think you are. We want you to help us bring him down. What do you say?"

My best poker face wasn't enough to conceal my surprise with what Special Agent Johnson had said. I quickly invited them inside so as to not attract any accidental attention to myself. As usual, Little T.J. was running around enthusiastically. This time, I allowed him to shake the hands of both Johnson and Samuels. After all, they may have been the perfect pawns to help get Angel back to me and in my good graces.

"Even if I knew what you two were talking about, why would you want him?" I inquired.

"Tell us everything you know about him. How long has he been trying to shake you down?"

"I know he's a cop. Harassed me and my crew a few times. Even had a couple of his boys in blue pull us over more than a few times! And for nothing! He's one of you guys, so why would you want to take him down?"

"You're wrong, Prentice. He's not one of us. He's a bad cop walking around in the streets with a badge that he doesn't deserve to be wearing. So, to answer your question, that's why we want to bring him down."

"So what's in it for me? Assuming I know what you are talking about."

"I'm going to make it real plain and easy for you, Prentice. We are in the position to let you skate by on everything you have done up to this point in our conversation. And you have done some things!"

"Oh really? Like what?"

"Why do you think no one has brought you in for the murder of Renaldo Dart, otherwise known as Preemo? Or your brother and father's old running partner, Trevor Diggs? What about all of those drug runs of yours to West Virginia? Georgia? New Jersey? Connecticut? That bogus front you call a trucking company? We could have you sitting in a cell right now with your brother for the rest of your miserable life, so I would strongly suggest you cooperate with us."

Undoubtedly, my demeanor had shifted from cool and calm to anxious and angry. I was furious because these two special agents knew just about everything I had been doing since my inception into my family's inner circle, and anxious because I could have been looking at life behind bars if I didn't give these two men what they wanted.

"Okay, I'm in. What exactly do you need me to do?"

David L.

"We were hoping you would cooperate and see things our way."

CHAPTER SEVENTEEN

I had a little over twenty-four hours left to take out Lincoln. He had become more of a liability now that the FBI was onto him. That made it me, the lettermen, and Angel's abductor who all wanted a piece of him. I almost felt sorry for him. Almost. He was the one who had no idea what he had gotten himself into.

"I have your money, but I can't meet you at the diner," I said to Lincoln over my cell phone.

"Why not?"

"You drive an unmarked vehicle and look the part of a cop. You have no idea how much heat I got last time we hooked up."

"So where then?"

"How 'bout over by the old warehouse downtown? You know, the one that almost burned down about a year and a half ago?"

"Off of Jay Street?"

"Yeah, that one."

"Come by yourself."

I had approximately one hour to meet up with Lincoln at our designated spot. One hour to do what I had been assigned to do.

But what about a possible set-up? That could have been one big ploy from the Feds AND Lincoln to bring me down. However, it was a chance in faith that I would have to follow in order to make it work. Only two things could happen: one, I would get set up by either Lincoln and the Feds; or two, everything would go according to plan, and by that time the following day, Angel would be safely in her apartment.

Special Agents Johnson and Samuels had me wired for extra precaution, and I had a gun that they didn't know about tucked away in my waistline just in case. Upon my arrival, Lincoln was already present and seated in his vehicle talking on his cell phone. I beeped my horn to get his attention and exited my ride.

"Let's make this quick," he said. "I've got me a little blonde-haired mistress waiting for me back at her place."

"Hold up. I need you to count my money in front of me. This way, you don't call me five minutes from now talkin' about how I shorted you."

"I'll take your word for it."

"I can't work like that. It won't take you but a couple of minutes."

Lincoln did just as I requested, even taking the time to make sure all of the money was in sequential order from lowest denomination to highest.

"You're a good business man," he said to me, while putting his newly-acquired money onto the passenger seat. "I almost hate to take your money like this sometimes."

I got a prompt through my wire from Special Agent Johnson to keep talking to him. Get him to incriminate himself further. I got Lincoln's attention just as he was getting ready to drive off.

"This hush money you're getting from me...you're supposed to give me the heads-up when the heat is comin' down on me, right?"

"That's correct. What's your point?"

"Well, I got two good crew members awaiting bail because no one gave them warning that the heat was comin' down on them! What's up with that?"

Lincoln didn't disappoint. He took the bait and responded to my inquiry just like I knew he would.

"The heat would've come down on you and your boys a long time ago if not for me. Remember that, Prentice. Or else you're going to find yourself without my services."

That was enough stalling on my part. If I had kept talking, he was bound to get a little suspicious. Besides, that should have been all the lettermen needed to make their bust. Now, all I needed to do was sit back and wait for the signal.

I quickly got back into my ride and travelled safely a few cars behind Lincoln to see what happened next. That was my money in his pockets, and I needed to know that retribution would commence shortly. He was getting ready to make his turn onto the Manhattan Bridge, and I didn't see Special Agents Johnson or Samuels anywhere. Then I did. They must have called for back-up, because two more squad cars merged onto the intersection of the bridge. One squad car turned immediately in front of Lincoln's car, promptly cutting him off.

"About damn time!" I said to myself, as I moved up closer to get a better view.

Two undercover officers got out of their vehicles and walked over to Lincoln. The traffic was quickly forming, so I quickly pulled over to safety and parked my ride so I could check out the festivities. Sure enough, Lincoln was being questioned by one of the officers, then handcuffed and led to one of the squad cars. Special Agents Johnson and Samuels were noticeably absent from the action and remained parked across the street. So, I took the time to find my way over to them.

"What do you want, kid? Go on home. You did good today. We got him."

"Man, f**k that! He's got my money, and I want it back!"

"Not gonna happen, kid," Samuels said. "That money is evidence now. Besides, with your track record, no judge in his right state of mind would even consider giving back blood money. Now go on home and wait for us to call you."

"So it's like that, huh? What makes you think someone from Lincoln's crew is not gonna step in and continue in his absence? And what's gonna happen to him?"

"Now you're worried about him? It's a little late for that now, don't you think? He's gonna be charged and hopefully sentenced for a long time. You won't have to worry about Lincoln or anyone else from his precinct extorting you or your little crew again. Now, get out of here before I bring you in, too!"

Fresh out on bail, Marley and Fredro were ordered to report directly to E-Black's apartment and wait for me to arrive. I had a lot to do and not much time to do it in. That was the day I was supposed to off Lincoln in order to satisfy my ransom obligations and get Angel back. The only problem was that Lincoln wouldn't be present. Not unless he somehow was released from detainment and was stupid enough to still take the ride over to Coney Island to make his appointment. It may not matter. Hopefully, whoever had Angel captive did not know what had transpired, and I would get either a phone call or another letter left on my windshield afterwards.

When I did finally show up to E-Black's place, Swift was also in attendance, followed shortly afterwards by Jackie.

"Who bailed y'all out?" I asked Marley and Fredro.

"I did," Swift interrupted. "You've been real sidetracked lately, so I took care of business for you…like a good lieutenant would do!"

It was a jab at me, but I deserved it after all of the secrecy and withholding of information I was responsible for. Besides, it was about time I filled everyone in before they heard about it from someone else. If the Feds had been tailing me and were aware of all of my comings and goings, I knew they would be tracking the whereabouts of my crew members, as well.

"I just came from a run-in with the lettermen," I said.

"What happened?" Jackie questioned.

"They busted Lincoln as he drove off from our appointment. They must have been following me the entire time."

"So no more Lincoln?" Swift asked.

"I guess not. At least for now anyway. But, we have more pressing matters. I'm supposed to meet him over by the aquarium in half an hour. The only problem is I don't have anyone to meet up with."

I instructed Marley and Fredro to go over to the projects that Tone stayed at and get some information on how he came into so much money. Word was that he was continuing to spread money around and snort up crazy amounts of coke. I needed to find out how he was doing it. And Marley and Fredro were the perfect ones to find out for me.

"Before y'all leave, whatever happened to Flash? How come he wasn't picked up, too?"

"You didn't tell him what we told you, Swift?" Marley said. "Your boy Flash is a mole for the cops! I knew there was something I didn't trust about him, but I couldn't put my finger on it."

"And how do you know this to be true?"

"'Cause he broke out just before we were picked up. He said something about making a quick stop at the corner bodega to get something to eat."

"Yeah? So? That makes him a mole?"

"No. What makes him a mole is when we were picked up by one-time, we caught him flagging down a cab as we rode by him in the backseat of the squad car!"

The time was ten o'clock Sunday night, and I arrived at the aquarium as directed to see what Angel's abductor would do next. My cell phone was in my hand so that I didn't miss any important calls alerting me to the next instructions. I was standing directly outside, hoping a move – any move – was made so that I could react accordingly. It was already raining slightly upon my arrival. However, the rain was now beginning to pick up in intensity.

"Whoever this mystery person is, they're late," I said to myself, while getting back into my ride to avoid getting wet from the downpour.

Ten more minutes went by without a sign of anyone. At approximately fifteen minutes after the hour, I got my first phone call from none other than Swift.

"Don't go anywhere, P. I've got one helluva surprise for you. Wait right there!"

I did as instructed, pulling out all of the correspondence from Angel's abductor and reading each letter over and over again for some possible clues. A few more minutes went by, and still no Swift…or anyone else for that matter. Then I got another call from Swift.

"Look across the street. Do you see a blue mini-van?"

Sure enough, there was a blue mini-van across from where I was parked. So, I promptly started my engine and made a U-turn, pulling up immediately behind it. Swift got out from the driver's side, followed soon after by Marley, Fredro, and Drac.

"What are y'all doin' here?" I blurted out.

"Take a look inside," Swift responded.

My eyes opened up as wide as they could when I opened the sliding door. Inside the van, ex crew member Tone was bound and gagged, and appeared to have been physically worked over by someone.

"Damn, he looks like he was in a war!" I said.

Marley and Fredro looked at each other and smiled. I didn't need any guess to figure out they had something to do with Tone's predicament.

"Where did y'all pick him up?" I asked.

Swift jumped in before either Marley or Fredro had a chance to respond.

"Marley and Fredro went up to the projects where Tone does most of his dealing, and just as they pulled up, they saw your boy Tone getting into this here mini-van. Then they followed him. But, that's not the best part."

"So then what? What happened next?"

"We followed him over to Gates Avenue," Fredro responded.

"That's when we called Swift to meet up with us over there because Tone just sat in the car for like thirty minutes, as if he was waiting for someone," Marley interjected.

"Let me tell it," Swift again interfered.

"To make a long story short, I get there and ya boy Tone walks into one of them buildings on Gates Ave. You remember going over there, right? Near the abandoned building connected to where we hooked up with Lord and Wise."

"Yeah? So? Get back to Tone's part in this whole thing."

"I'm getting to that. So, anyway, we wait in our ride to see what Tone is up to. He finally gets out, but not before being waved into the building by two men wearing hoods. They were Lord and Wise!"

"So he's connected to them? But what about the letter? Angel? My fifty thousand!"

Swift proceeded to take the gag out of Tone's mouth, while at the same time, motioning everyone back into the mini-van to avoid being detected and to avoid the rainfall that was coming down even harder.

"Let him explain everything," Swift responded. "This is

gonna blow your mind!"

"If I tell you everything you need to know, will you release me, P?" Tone questioned.

"If everything checks out and goes the way it's supposed to, I may actually do that. But, first things first. Where's Angel?"

"She's being kept in a basement next to the abandoned building on Gates. Lord and Wise have had her there handcuffed to the bed since they had me pick her up seven days ago. Once a day, they have me go there and check up on her. Feed her. Make sure she's safe and everything."

"Why?"

"Because he wants a monopoly. You thought all this time the two of you could peacefully co-exist without anything going down? Lord has been plotting on bringing your family down before Innocent ever got put away for life! When I bounced on you, Wise was the first person to reach out to me."

"And Preemo?"

"Wise played the both of you. He was in Preemo's ear the entire time, telling him how you were comin' to look for him. Then when you said you wanted a piece of Preemo, Wise got excited and figured he could get a two-for-one deal because y'all would be too busy going after one another. Even Trevor got caught up in his scheme. He was all up in his ear talkin' about how he needed to turn on your family because he never got the respect he deserved from your pops. You think you're the man, P? Wise more than doubled his loot in the last few months. Now he's the top drug runner in the whole five boroughs. I'll put my life on that!"

"You may have to!"

"I'm worth more alive to you right now than ever before. Turning my back on you was personal, but this here is business. Let me help you get your girl back and I can be on my way. You won't ever have to see my ugly face again. That's my word."

"Right now?

"Right now."

CHAPTER EIGHTEEN

"I swear if you don't stop your whining, I'm going to shut you up permanently!" I said, referring to Tone, who was now trying to get one of us to untie him. "Where's the building?" I questioned.

"We're almost there. Turn here," Swift responded. "It's down by the bottom on the right-hand side."

"Are you sure no one is going to be there?" I asked, looking at Tone.

"I know that for a fact. Lord and Wise are on an out-of-town job in Delaware. They won't be back until tomorrow."

"Pull up right here," I said to Swift. "I don't trust him. At least this way, if they're inside, we can catch them off guard. Drac, are you packin'?"

I got the head nod from him, as he lifted up his shirt slightly so I could see the handle of a gun protruding from his waist.

"Even if he wasn't, you know we stay with the heat!" Marley added.

Typical bravado coming from a couple of kids not even out of their teenage years. I had done some "digging" on both of my young guns, and both had lived very harsh, dysfunctional lives.

Both came up in foster care from a very early age, and both had mothers that were still very much involved in crack cocaine and any other drug they could get their hands on to maintain their high. Neither of them ever knew their father, and neither of them made it through junior high school.

"So now what, boss?" Drac questioned.

"Now we enter. Y'all stay here and look after my investment," I said to Marley and Fredro. "He may prove useful after all."

Marley reached into Tone's jeans and pulled out keys that opened up the basement door which would lead me directly to Angel. The first flight of stairs on the way down was very old. So, I watched my every step for fear of falling straight down to the bottom of the staircase.

"This could be a trap for all we know," Swift said timidly.

"This ain't no trap," I responded. "Drac, be ready to pull out just in case…"

Both Drac and I watched as Swift fumbled the key ring, dropping them twice onto the cold cement floor of the basement. When we entered the apartment, it was nothing like I had envisioned it. The basement apartment was nicely furnished, the air conditioning had been left on, and I could detect the faint scent of a candle burning.

"This place is nicer than my pad," Swift said jokingly.

"I don't care how nice you think it is, Swift. Lord is going to pay for this. Mark my words!"

"WHO IS THAT?" a familiar voice asked.

The voice belonged to Angel, and I followed her voice to a dimly-lit back room. Sure enough, she was handcuffed to a bedpost – tears filling up her eyes from what looked to be excitement by my presence.

"Stay still. Let me get you out of this," I said, but had no luck. "Damn, Drac! How the hell are we going to get these handcuffs off of her?"

"Let me try!" Swift said, pulling out his nine millimeter.

"Fool, are you crazy? And accidentally shoot her?" I responded.

"We're going to have to break down the frame from underneath. Look here. This is how they were able to keep her trapped here and not be able to lift up the bed to make her escape," Drac said.

He then proceeded to show us the bottom of the bed frame, which was nailed down to the foundation of the basement floor. It took a few moments, but just as promised, he was able to release Angel immediately into my waiting arms. Thoughts of her cheating on me with that so-called high school friend of hers didn't even come to mind. All that mattered was that she was safe.

Angel took a deep breath upon reaching the outside of the building. After all, it was her first time outdoors in seven days. Everyone else was in the van, and with my first real few minutes alone with her, I had to ask the obvious.

"Did any of them touch you anywhere? You know – sexually?"

"They didn't rape me, if that's what you're asking. Is that what you were worried about this entire time? What about if they killed me, Prentice? Your child?"

"I'm sorry. It's just…"

"Just what?"

"I've been doing a lot of thinking, and you were right all along."

"About what?"

"This life. This isn't for me. I swear, as soon as this is over, I'm going down south to start a new life. Will you come with me? You and the baby? Say you will go. I've already made up my mind and accepted a job down there paying good money. It's a chance for the two of us to begin fresh, new lives. Don't answer right this minute, but think it over. Sleep on it if you have to."

"Okay, I will. Now let's get the hell out of here. I don't ever

David L.

want to come to this part of Brooklyn again for as long as I live!"

Back at E-Black's apartment, the real fun began. The next day when Lord and whoever else he went down to Delaware with returned, there was going to be a full-scale war. Although she came unwillingly, I was able to convince Angel to stay at my brother's house, at least for the night. It was way too dangerous for her to return to her apartment, and I had to make sure she was well protected. The following morning, I would send all of them to a hotel to lay low for a few weeks.

Drac was also there, and in a few minutes, I would be calling my sister to stay at her fiancé's house. Tone was still whining about being released and returning back to the projects in which he dwelled. I had other plans for him, though.

"I let you go and you leave out of Brooklyn...probably never to return? No way!" I said.

"What should we do with him, P?" Swift asked.

"We can take him over to my old apartment and leave him tied up there. That will give him some insight into how it feels to be helpless. Everyone knows I've been staying at Innocent's house, so he should be safe there for the time being."

"Can't we torture him just a little?" Marley questioned, already knowing instinctively the answer to his question.

"Sometimes you can get more with tact than torture," I responded. "So, Tone, what else are you leaving out? You're a dead man if Lord and the rest of his crew catch up to you, so you may want to fly straight. You might as well come clean with me and tell me what's really good."

"What do you mean? I told you everything. There's nothing more to tell."

"I'm not too sure of that. Has anyone searched him for weapons? Or even bothered to take his cell phone from him so he can't sneak any phone calls or text anyone?"

I took it upon myself to do the dirty work and go into his pants pockets. Sure enough, he had a cell phone and a razor blade that I immediately confiscated. A familiar-looking business card fell out as I placed my hand into his back pants pocket. It was the same business card that was handed to me by my two favorite lettermen from the FBI. Instead of questioning Tone about what he was doing with their business card and run the risk of telling on myself, I played it off and placed it back into his pocket. Also in his pocket was my sister's address.

"So my sister was next?" I asked, stating the obvious.

"Yeah. Lord was comin' for you hard. Fifty thousand for your girl and another fifty for your sister. If that didn't put you out of business, he was going to have me and a few others go after your nephew next. He figured since he was unable to collect on your pop's bounty, he would make the money off of you instead."

"And how did any of this benefit you? I know he broke you off with something."

"Yeah, he did. Twenty thousand a job. But, I swear, P…I made sure I told him to treat everyone nice. Not to hurt anyone. Why you think Angel is even still alive? That is the God honest truth!"

Now everyone connected to me had to be contacted…or face possible retaliation from Lord and his crew. I took a moment to get my thoughts together and then instructed everyone to carry out my requests. Marley and Fredro had left the apartment to intercept Angel's roommate at her place of employment to ensure her safety and recommend to her an alternate place of residence temporarily. Drac, Crystal, T.J., and Angel should have been arriving at a hotel of their choice within the hour. And Swift? He was going to stay with his off again, on again girl out in Starrett City until everything died down.

David L.

"We need to talk NOW!" I said to Special Agent Samuels, talking over one of the very few working payphones left in all of Brooklyn.

"So you finally decided to take us up on our offer?"

"Man, forget about all that! I've got two words for you: Tone Greene!"

"What about him? He was one of your old runnin' partners and we saw an excellent opportunity to squeeze some information from him. Especially since you wouldn't cooperate with us," Samuels explained. "Now get the hell off the streets before someone trying to collect on that bounty sees you. Come down to the Promenade downtown. We need to have a sit-down."

With nothing more to lose, I made my way down to the Promenade, but not before calling Angel to check up on her. Drac picked up the line and informed me that she was asleep. She and I hadn't had a real chance to talk about what transpired between the two of us since her abduction, and I wanted to tell her that all of the indiscretion was finally behind me. I was ready to move on and make an honest man out of myself.

Special Agents Johnson and Samuels were already at the Promenade upon my arrival, and we began walking. It was now dusk and I could clearly see the lights from the Brooklyn Bridge across from me emanating from the reflection in the water below.

"So what was so important that you had to get me down here and away from my family?" I asked.

"You may not have a family if you don't do as we say," Agent Samuels replied with a serious tone. "You're a marked man. I know you know that already."

"Yeah, I do. But what can you do for me? I already helped you bring down Lincoln."

"Yeah, you helped us bring him in, but you will eventually have to testify. And that's small potatoes. We want Lord and

Wise just as much as you do. So much that we're willing to look the other way so you can do whatever you need to do to bring him down. You do that and we won't give you any more problems."

"Let me get this straight. You want ME to bring down Lord? And you aren't going to do nothing? Let me off the hook? What's the catch?"

"No catch. You think you're big-time? You're nothing compared to what Lord and the rest of his men are pulling in weekly. Try over fifty thousand a week! You went to school, right? So then, you know how much that is! We're willing to let you make your little pocket change for the real catch...and that's Lord. So what do you say?"

Even at dusk time, I knew Special Agents Johnson and Samuels must have noticed me smiling about their latest offer. Unbeknownst to them, I had already found my replacement in the drug game and would be legit immediately after I settled my score with Lord.

"I'm in. I take him out and I get no resistance from you, right?"

"That's right, but mention either of our names and I swear..."

"Let me stop you right there. First of all, I'm leaving town first chance I get. I'm leaving these streets for you to clean up. I'm done with it. Secondly, do I look stupid? You come around my house trying to get in good with me. Then you're feeding information to one of my known enemies, and then to top it off, you don't want me to talk? Johnson and Samuels probably aren't even your real names! What kind of promotion did you get for bringing down Lincoln? And now Lord is next? Trust me when I say you will NEVER have to worry about me trying to implicate either one of you in any of my nonsense!"

CHAPTER NINETEEN

"**W**hat are you still doing here?" I questioned, referring to one of the employees at my family's trucking company.

"Working late trying to figure out these books of yours," she responded.

The voice belonged to Robin, one of my most diligent young upstarts who recently began working here about six months ago. She was interning as our official accountant and also using this opportunity to pay her way through college. I had taken a minor liking to her for some reason. Not of attraction, but for sentimental purposes. The other twenty plus employees had all been there before I officially took over. However, I personally interviewed Robin and put her under my wing. And she had been living up to her potential ever since.

"Nothing adds up, Prentice. I don't know how you've been able to get by for so long."

"Well, go 'head and do your thing. I won't get in your way. I just have to go into the back and check on some things."

What I really had to do was go into the back room and remove anything that could incriminate me, and at the same time, have enough pocket cash on me for when I left New York. I was in the middle of a serious scandal, and the best thing for me to do was get the f**k out of dodge! For all I knew, those two lettermen would be coming after me with the quickness after they brought down Lord and his crew. Little did they know they wouldn't find me. Not in New York anyway!

I was now in the back room, which only I had the key to. There was a safe on the wall, and inside, about seventy to eighty thousand dollars in cash. Enough to get myself situated down in West Virginia until I could figure out a way to sell my fifty percent stake in the company, the other half now owned by my sister Tammy. Just my luck, there were no bags of any kind that I could place the money into. So, I did the next best thing and pulled out the plastic lining from the garbage to place my cash into. Not the perfect remedy, but it would suffice – for the time being anyway.

I could see the back of Robin as she was perched on her chair, viewing about twenty-five sheets of paper scattered all across her desk. She looked frustrated, and at the same time, appeared very alluring with her legs crossed and her hand massaging the back of her neck.

"Is there anything I can help you with?" I asked.

"Unless you can magically fix these numbers, probably not. I may be here all night trying to balance out these spreadsheets."

Even her voice was alluring. And the way she said "spreadsheets" was damn near intoxicating!

"What do you have there?" she questioned, referring to the garbage bag I was holding in my hand.

"This here? Nothing. I've got some old files from last year that I'm going to take home and shred."

"They must be some pretty important files, because I haven't seen you here in weeks!"

"You look tired. Why don't you go home and get some rest. And it's too late to be calling a cab. I can give you a ride home."

Robin accepted my offer, but only after spending the next few minutes looking over some more random papers on her desk. Enough time for me to go out to my car and place my small fortune inside the trunk.

"I might not have offered you a ride home if I knew you lived all the way out here in Far Rockaway!" I said jokingly.

"I'm so sorry to take you out of your way. Can I interest you in something to drink? Eat?"

My professional ethnics told me to decline. However, I hadn't had a good meal in a minute. Between Angel and me not on speaking terms, and Crystal going out almost every night to meet up with her new man, I had been eating out about six out of the seven days of the week.

"Depends on what you have to eat," I responded.

"A little bit of everything. It was my birthday yesterday, so I invited a few friends over and made a whole bunch of food. Come on in."

I respectfully obliged the request, but not before promising to pick up a little birthday present for her of my own in the near future, along with a complimentary day off with pay.

The inside of Robin's apartment smelled like potpourri, and there were unlit candles in just about every room I entered. The television was on, which led me to believe someone else was also in the apartment. My gun had been tucked away on my side since my run-in with the lettermen, and I felt for it to make sure it was still on me. For all I knew, being there could have been a set-up. It wouldn't have been the first time.

"If you're wondering about the television, don't worry about it. I keep it on when I leave the apartment so that potential burglars think twice before breaking in. Pretty smart, don't cha' think?"

I nodded my head in agreement and then had a seat on the couch. I could hear the beeping of the microwave and the smell of something very appealing. Robin returned from the kitchen with spaghetti and steak – one of my favorite meal combinations.

"I like to watch movies with my meal," Robin uttered, inserting a disc into her DVD player.

"Oh snap! You got *Cooley High*! What do you know about that?" I said, referring to Robin's age.

Although neither of us was around during that era, I still had her beat by at least two or three years.

"My father who passed away recently put me onto this. His DVD collection is crazy!"

"We have a lot in common. My father passed away too recently."

We both got relatively quiet from talking about our recent loss and sat back and enjoyed the movie of the moment. Before I knew it, my eyes started getting heavy, and a couple of times, I caught myself nodding off only to be awakened by Robin. After several minutes went by, having fallen asleep, I was totally oblivious to whatever was going on in the movie. I was prematurely awakened by Robin who, when I opened my eyes, was kissing me tenderly on my neck. The combination of not getting any for so long and Robin's beauty made it even harder to tell her to stop. So, I didn't. Instead, she continued in frequency and intensity. Before long, she had her hand between my legs, daring me to reciprocate. And I did. Now we were kissing and groping each other with even more ferociousness, all while beginning to remove each other's clothing. Our lovemaking initially began on the couch, but we soon found ourselves on the bedroom floor. Everything else from that moment on happened so quickly that before I knew it, I was in my car and driving onto the highway ramp to head back to my brother's house.

Back at my old apartment, Tone was still bound and gagged. Marley and Fredro, who were left there to keep an eye on him, were keeping themselves occupied by playing a basketball game on my Playstation system in the back room.

"Anything new?" I asked.

"Nah. Everything's been quiet, P," Marley replied.

"Except Tone's cell phone keeps going off. I think it's the alarm or something."

"You dummy!" I responded, reaching for Tone's cell phone that was placed on a nearby table. "That's no alarm. Those are missed calls, and the calls are coming from Lord! Did either of you even bother to look at the screen?"

I proceeded to take the towel out of Tone's mouth in order for him to speak.

"I'm gonna put the phone to your ear so you can speak with Lord. Tell him you were distracted by one of your gold digging women. He's probably gonna want to meet up with you so he can get his cut of my fifty thousand. If he does, tell him you had to leave it at the same apartment y'all kept Angel captive."

I called the number back, and as instructed, Tone followed through. Just as I expected, the first thing Lord wanted to know was if his money was delivered.

"One more thing…" I remarked.

"Yeah?"

"What were you planning on doing with the Fed's number in your back pocket?"

"Oh that? That was insurance in case Lord tried to play me for my loot. Those Fed boys told me that if I helped them rat you and Lord out, I could pocket a percentage of the bounty money that Lord had placed on you. I got warrants all throughout the five boroughs. They told me if I played along, they would make them go away."

"Those slick bastards!" I said to myself.

They were playing us all along. Divide and conquer. And each and every one of us fell for it. Well, I had a couple of tricks up my sleeve, too. Although I didn't trust Tone no further than I could throw him, he was my bait to Lord. Afterwards, I could discard of him like the expendable and worthless slime that he was.

"Give me your wallet," I said.

"Whatcha want with my wallet?" Tone responded.

"Insurance. If you try to tip Lord off when you get there, don't bother tryin' to return home. You do and you're dead."

I had enough guns in my ride to start a borough war. With me were Drac, E-Black, and Swift. Jackie and her girls were in another car down the block, playing lookout for when Lord and his crew arrived. Marley and Fredro were in the van with Tone as he headed over to the same building Angel was held captive to meet up with Lord and whoever else may be with him. Tone and I communicated through our cell phones, and he had been instructed to enter with both Marley and Fredro by his side. When Lord arrived that day, Drac, Swift, and I would already be inside and ready to make our ambush. Neither Lord nor any of his crew knew Marley and Fredro were connected with me, so they should prove to be pretty useful, while at the same time being able to keep a close eye on Tone in the event he tried anything.

"Who are these kids?" Lord questioned, referring to Marley and Fredro.

"They're some of my new recruits," Tone responded.

"Send them home. This is big-boy business."

"Lord is outside the building talking to Tone right now," Jackie told me through her cell phone.

"Good. We're ready for him."

Jackie also informed me that along with Lord was five other individuals, all driving their own cars. Two remained stationary in their rides while Lord and another individual remained outside talking to Tone. My guess was the other individual was none other than his right-hand man, Wise.

"So where's my money?" Lord asked Tone.

"Inside. I have it stashed away under the bed."

"And the girl?"

"She's still tied up to the bed. She ain't goin' nowhere."

I could hear movement, soon followed by footsteps walking down a flight of steps. The doorknob was starting to turn, as the three of us cocked our weapons back and got ready for action.

"GET ON THE FLOOR!" I screamed as the first person entered.

That person was Wise, who quickly gave in to my demand and dropped to the ground. Unfortunately for me, Lord did not enter with him.

"Watch where you aim that thing!" E-Black said, moving out of our range of fire.

Swift and Drac kept their weapons pointed towards Wise, while I reached into my pocket to answer my phone.

"GET OUT THERE NOW!" Jackie yelled into the receiver. "I think Lord was just tipped off!"

"This is f**ked up!" I said to Drac and Swift. "Lord is still out there, and he's gonna get away! Y'all stay here with Wise, and if he moves…"

"I'll blast his a**! Swift said, cutting me off.

I quickly ran up the basement steps, while at the same time instructing Jackie on what to do next.

"It's a set-up!" I could hear Lord saying to his other crew members as I made my way out of the building.

With gun in hand, I began firing at whoever was not down

with me. As soon as Marley and Fredro saw me exit the building, they pulled out their own weapons and began firing. Tone got down on the pavement to avoid getting shot. Lord was making a run for it while firing his own weapon towards me, and the other remaining members of his crew that remained in their vehicles began to drive towards him.

"Stay in the car! Don't try to be a hero!" I told Jackie, while getting down on all fours to avoid getting hit with any strays.

Both Marley and Fredro ducked behind a parked car to avoid getting hit, also. Lord, although noticeably limping from catching one in the leg, was now in one of his crew member's rides as they all drove off to apparent safety. Marley, holding his side, also appeared to have been hit. Drac, Swift, and E-Black were now outdoors, blood all over Swift's boots.

"What happened to you?" I questioned, talking to Swift.

"Your boy Wise made a move towards me. So, I took him out."

"He's no use to us dead. I told you about being so damn trigger happy."

"I know. My fault."

"Lord isn't going to take this lying down. Let's get the hell outta here and regroup," Drac insisted.

"We will, but before we leave, there's some unfinished business that needs to be addressed."

I removed my piece from my waist and pointed it towards Tone, who was totally oblivious that I knew he was the one that tipped Lord to the fact that he was set up.

BANG!

One pointblank shot to the head was all it took. Tone dropped lifeless to the ground in front of us.

"Now we can get outta here," I said.

CHAPTER TWENTY

"**Y**ou're just talkin' scared right now, P. Give it a few days of thought and get back out there. Everything will work itself out."

That was my sister Tammy talking to me from her fiancé's place. When word got out that she was next in line to be abducted, she quickly packed everything up and decided to move in with him permanently. She was going on and on about my decision to relocate to West Virginia and part ways with the family business – both the legal AND illegal aspects of it.

"My mind is made up. I'm on my way over to the hotel right now to inform Crystal and the others. They're supposed to all meet up with me there so I can introduce E-Black as the new person in charge."

"And the trucking company?"

"I've been meaning to talk to you about that…"

"What about?"

"I want you to take over the day-to-day operations. It's gonna need someone with a forceful personality that can whip my drivers into shape…and you're the perfect person for the job."

Crystal, T.J., and Angel were all staying over at the Radisson Hotel located in upper Manhattan where they could be out of harm's way. Before my arrival there, I needed to stop at the barbershop. The same one I had been frequenting since my father stopped shaping me up when I was twelve.

"What up, fellas!" I said exuberantly, as I seated myself in the owner Milton's chair.

No wait. No worries. That's what an extra twenty dollars got you in my neighborhood. Every other chair in the shop was occupied, and on a beautiful Saturday afternoon at one of the most happening barbershops in Brooklyn, what could you expect?

"Yo, Milt, this might be your last time seeing me up in your chair," I said discreetly. "I'm leaving this madness for rest and relaxation. I'm movin' down south."

Milton gave me his best wishes and fixed me up with my signature cut.

"You got beef with the cops, P?" a nearby barber questioned.

"Not that I know of. Why?"

"'Cause there were a couple of cops here looking for you 'bout an hour ago. Showed us a picture of you and everything. Said they would be back."

My heart began to race and my palms were sweaty. They must have been some of Lincoln's boys looking for some payback. It made sense. The lettermen told me that I would eventually have to testify, so Lincoln must have sent some of his boys to make sure I didn't make it to the trial.

Just as I hit Milton off with another ten spot for hooking me up, a couple more individuals walked into the shop. It was a couple of old acquaintances that my brother used to do business with before he was locked up. Their names were Shakim and Prince.

"What up, P!" Shakim said. "Heard you've been doin' some big things in these parts."

"Nothing too big. Just handlin' business, that's all. What's up with you?"

"Nothing much. Just got out the joint a few days ago. Maybe we can get down soon on some work down the line."

"Yeah, no doubt. We'll talk."

Milton motioned me back over to him and beckoned me not to turn around, while acting like he was putting the final touch on my shapeup.

"Those clowns were in here earlier today and asked a couple of my customers if they had seen you around. I overheard something about a bounty out on your head. I think they may be tryin' to collect. Get the hell out of here."

"You don't have to tell me twice. Do me a favor and call this number," I said, handing him a business card that I pulled from my pocket. "Ask for E-Black. Tell him I'll be there as soon as possible and to hold me down. He'll understand."

I made my way for the door, but I was again stopped by Shakim and Prince.

"Where you goin' in such a hurry?" Prince questioned.

"I got an appointment on the other side of town I have to follow up on. I'll catch up with y'all some other time."

I walked around the corner to where my ride was parked, and as soon as I turned the ignition, a red Nissan Sentra rolled up on the side of me.

"Lord sends his regards," the driver said, revealing a handgun, and then he aimed it towards me.

No shots were fired, probably because of the time of day and the number of witnesses in the general area, but either way, I immediately floored the gas pedal to make my escape. From my rearview mirror, I could see Shakim and Prince in front of the barbershop orchestrating the entire caper. They too were getting into their cars, probably to get in on the chase.

No rookie to a chase, I quickly maneuvered my way onto the nearest two-way street and drove through a couple of red lights. Even if I eluded my pursuers, it was too risky that I might get noticed by five-0. So, I pulled into someone's driveway just in time to watch my pursuer drive past me. It wasn't until several minutes later that I mustered up the nerve to make my departure and continue my destination to the Radisson.

"I wanted to take this time to let everyone know that I'm relocating to West Virginia. I can't do this anymore. I'm not built for this life. E-Black is taking over for me, and everything should go through him."

The look on everyone's face was priceless, except for E-Black, who was the only one that knew this day was coming... just not so soon. I handed E-Black about twelve thousand in cash so everyone's room would be paid for through the rest of the week. Everyone was somewhat disappointed, but not nearly as disappointed as Swift. Out of everyone else, he had taken it the worst.

"So you're gonna sell us all out just like that?" he said.

I reminded Swift that I was brought into the business by my brother and father and never really wanted to participate. I shared with him my former dream of one day playing professional football. I may have not been able to change the past, but I could still influence my future. I even confided that I might register for school when I got down south.

Next, I pulled Angel into the bathroom for some one-on-one time. Our first alone time in what seemed to be an eternity.

"I want you to come with me. You and the baby. You asked me before to leave this life and it took some time, but I've finally figured out that you were right all along. So, once again, I'm asking you...will you come with me?"

"You're asking me to just up and leave everyone that I

know. I don't know if I can do that so easily. I'm going to need some time to think about it."

"I understand. Unfortunately, I don't have that luxury. I've got people after me. Dangerous people. Crooked cops. FBI. You name it. And they will come after you next. They already have once before."

I left Angel in her thoughts to process what I had just said to her. Between my bank accounts and the money from the safe, I had a little less than two hundred thousand to start over from scratch.

Now gathered in the living room area of the suite with everyone else, Swift was still visibly frustrated. One, because of my abrupt exit, and two, he was not put in the position to run things in my absence. He had been loyal, and before I made my leave, I would pull him over to the side and share my reasoning with him.

"I need you to stay focused, kid. I need you to understand why I'm doing this. You and I…we come from the same hood, but we've always led very different lifestyles. I'm not going to tell you to leave this life, because I know you ain't gonna listen anyway, but…"

"You're not getting all emotional on me, are you? The last thing I need to see is a grown-a** man cry!" Swift said.

"Nah, nothing like that. I'm just saying be careful. Lord isn't going to stop until he gets his revenge. You know that like I know it. I don't want to get a call from Tammy telling me that you got taken out…like all the rest. That's all I'm sayin'."

"No doubt. To tell you the truth, I've always kinda been envious of you, man. You got something with Angel that many people wish they had. Go begin that life of yours. Get the f**k out of New York while you can! Give me six months, and I'll catch up with you down there. That's on the real!"

"You serious? If you are, I got a job waiting for you."

"I'm as serious as cancer! Six months and I'm out."

Hearing Swift finally talking some sense had done a lot for

my morale. He was finally beginning to understand that the life we were living would only lead him down two roads: jail or death. And I wouldn't want him to have to experience either.

Everyone now knew my plan and that I would be driving into the sunset early the following Sunday morning to avoid the weekend congestion on I-95. There was just one more person I needed to see before I departed.

I made the four and a half hour drive to where Innocent was locked up and barely had thirty minutes for visiting time. Although it wouldn't be my last visit, it was a grim reminder that face-to-face time with my brother would soon be greatly decreased due to my relocation.

As usual, Innocent arrived in his prison-issued grey uniform. He was clean shaven and much more relaxed than during our previous visits.

"I know why you're here today," he said. "I don't blame you. Go on and live your life, lil' bro. You won't get any complaints from me. Just make sure you don't forget about me."

My eyes filled up with tears. Not because I was leaving, but because of what was just said. Words I never thought I would hear. Maybe it was a combination of the reality of doing life in prison. Maybe my brother found Allah. Who knows? Whatever it was, I was completely at awe at his change of disposition. This was the same person that used to pressure me into getting into the family business.

"I leave tomorrow morning," I said.

"By yourself?"

"Not quite sure. Either way, I'm going. If I don't, I'll be dead in a week."

"I know. That's the real reason I want you to go. The streets are talking, kid. I'm getting word from in here that if you're found, you're as good as dead. So, leave. Get the hell out of New York. You have my blessing."

I confided in Innocent that having his blessing meant more to me than he could ever imagine. In my absence, I was leaving many unanswered questions behind for E-Black, Swift, and the others to figure out without me.

Without my testimony, what would be Lincoln's fate?

With me out of New York, would Lord continue his onslaught on E-Black and the others, or would things die down?

Would Tammy be able to hold the trucking company down, or would everything crumble around her?

And what about Special Agents Samuels and Johnson? Would they continue their divide and conquer tactics on everyone they came in contact with, or would they shift their attention to the next up and coming drug lord of New York?

In due time, all of the above questions would be addressed. Then and only then would there be closure…and for some – peace of mind.

EPILOGUE
ONE YEAR LATER...

As expected, my sister **Tammy** has taken the family trucking company to the next level. In the last three months alone, sales have been up fifteen percent; she has purchased three more trucks and hired four more staff to assist with the interstate runs. No longer is the trucking company a front for illegal trafficking. Tammy runs a legit business and is looking to expand again in the near future. She has hired **Robin**, the intern I had the impromptu one-night stand with, as the full-time accountant. Robin oversees all of the company's financial transactions, and her office is almost equal in size to Tammy's office. More importantly, Tammy and her loser fiancé are now married, and they are expecting their first child in about five months. Tammy and her husband have relocated out to Hempstead, New York, and own a modest two-family home that includes a very large backyard, front porch, and music studio. Although Tammy's husband sometimes helps out at the trucking company, he's still mainly supported by Tammy's income.

E-Black continues to run the business that my pops began so many years ago. However, E-Black primarily runs his operation out of his baby mother's apartment and utilizes local talent in the neighborhood to do his dirty work. He hasn't been seen by any of his crew members in over a month, and reportedly, he overindulges in alcohol and over-the-counter medications. The reason? About two months ago, E-Black was shot in his spine by an individual reportedly known to have been associated with Lord. The bullet pierced his spine, paralyzing him from the waist down. He's presently receiving physical therapy for his condition.

Lord is presently being detained at a maximum-secure prison in Ohio. About a month after my departure, Lord and a few of his crew members tried to bully their way into an Ohio territory and were run out by some of the more notorious locals. About a week later, Lord and his crew returned with guns drawn and shot up a local nightclub. Six people were seriously injured and three were murdered in the backlash. Lord was granted leniency due to his testimony towards his other crew members, some of who were given life sentences. However, the majority received sentences in which they will be up for parole within twenty to thirty years.

Without my testimony, **Lincoln** got off on all charges with nothing more than a slap on the wrist. He was transferred to an office job within his old precinct and primarily works nine to five, pushing a pencil for most of the day. The court proceedings were very lengthy and played a pivotal part in the demise of his marriage. After thirteen years of marriage, his wife filed for divorce due to alleged infidelity on his part. Along with the divorce, his former wife received custody of their two children as well as a very lucrative alimony payout. Lincoln's crew continues to try their luck at extorting neighborhood drug dealers. However, many of them have been shut down due to ongoing FBI sting operations.

Special Agents **Johnson** and **Samuels** continue to utilize their unconventional ways on aspiring drug lords. In the last year alone, they were able to get convictions on over two dozen wannabe kingpins throughout the five boroughs and neighboring states. Last month, both agents received commendations from the mayor for their ongoing bravery and above-and-beyond practices to decrease the level of drug sales in the state of New York. To date, no one is aware of their underlying tactics or their subversive attempts to gain the upper hand on rival drug lords.

Fredro and **Marley** were both picked up by undercover detectives about a month ago for drug-related charges, and unable to make bail, they remain locked up at Bridges Detention Center in the Bronx. They are both looking at about a year and a half to three years, but are expected to get their sentences reduced because of their age. Their public defender is seeking to have them placed in a juvenile residential treatment center far away from Brooklyn in order for them to get the services they need to eventually lead productive, positive lives.

Jackie and her two partners still occasionally strip at various clubs throughout the five boroughs and recently began starring in various rap music videos. Over the last year, all three have starred in over a dozen videos and have grossed close to six figures doing so. Jackie plans to open a gentlemen's club somewhere in downtown Brooklyn with her portion of the proceeds within the next year.

Crystal moved in with her boyfriend in Flushing, Queens and lives a very ordinary lifestyle. She does hair on the weekends and is constantly on the phone with my sister to get business tips on how to open up her own beauty salon. Like a true good woman, she keeps in touch with my brother and sends him miscellaneous gifts monthly to make his life behind bars that much more tolerable. **T.J.** is as precocious as I remember him, and according to Crystal, he looks more like Innocent every waking day. He's in a gifted class for kids with exceptional intelligence and is presently at the top of his class in academic achievement.

Drac no longer involves himself in any illegal activities and has totally changed his life around in a more positive direction. With the money he saved throughout his business dealings with Innocent and me, he purchased a brownstone in Harlem where he now resides with his son's mother and her seven-year-old son from a previous relationship. They are to be married in three weeks and are expecting another child. Drac is very much involved in his local church and coaches his son on the church's youth baseball team.

Swift wanted desperately to get out of the streets, but fate somehow always drove him back into it. He and I remained in close contact throughout the last year, and he promised that after one more interstate run to Connecticut for a huge payoff, he was going to come down my way and work for me. He did make the trip to Connecticut. However, he never made it back home. Immediately after collecting his product from a customer, he was mercilessly gunned down in broad daylight. He was pronounced dead moments later.

And **me**? I'm living the good life in West Virginia and have regular telephone contact with Innocent at least twice a month, or whenever he has extra phone privileges. He's a model prisoner and has even obtained employment within the prison mailroom. Although he will never see freedom in his lifetime, Innocent recently began tutoring incoming prisoners and is a mentor for those struggling with adapting to prison life. I, on the other hand, have a nine-month-old son named Trenton, in dedication to my brother, and a loving fiancé of my own – **Angel**. Yep, that's correct. Angel made that road trip with me and also works part-time at the restaurant I manage from time to time. Angel is in school working on her Bachelor's degree in social work, and I have also re-enrolled in school, although it doesn't begin until next semester. My life is blessed, but doesn't come without baggage. But, that's what makes us all unique in our own distinctive way.

THE END?

A WORD FROM DAVID L.

I would like for all of my books to be as addictive as the deadliest drug ever conceived – minus the harmful side effects and dire consequences. I believe I am close to that prophecy. My passion and purpose to that is of biblical proportions.

A word of caution: I will win over both your heart and confidence…and soon enough become your favorite author. That is both certain and promised. Please don't mistake my confidence for arrogance. Call it for what it is. .excellence of execution.

And to all the naysayers, I told you that I was going to drop a book every year. As you are reading this, I am a perfect 4 out of 4! Look out for Book #5 coming to a bookstore near you!

I have spoken… and so it shall be. Quoth the GOD.

Nevermore.

"TELL THE WORLD MY NAME!"

ACKNOWLEDGEMENTS

A special shout out to my entire family – both biological and personally hand-picked – supportive friends, casual acquaintances, and anyone else who feels they should be included here. Deep down, you know if you truly belong here! If you've never picked up a David L. book, then the answer is most likely no!

And a special recognition and salute to all the book clubs, media outlets, and publicity engines that has shown me love throughout the years; all the readers of my books that I've touched somehow; event coordinators that have booked me for events and given me premium location space to showcase my work at their venues.

All praises due to the most merciful GOD

R.I.P. to my brother from another mother – Andre "Dre 5000" Stoddard. You will never be forgotten. Peace and blessings until we cross paths again.

R.I.P. to my beautiful and dear cousin – Nicola. Your beautiful face will be forever etched in my heart.

R.I.P. to my Aunt Zoe (Ms. Francis) for the many times you put food in my stomach and watched on as I ran aimlessly around your house during my younger years.

ORDER FORM

Mail all payments and correspondence to:
TOTAL PACKAGE PUBLICATIONS, LLC
C/O DAVID L.
P.O. BOX 3237
MOUNT VERNON, NY 10553
www.totalpackagepublications.com

Name: _____

Address: _____

City/State/Zip: _____

Email: _____

TITLE	PRICE	QUANTITY
Over Your Dead Body	$15.00	
Chalk Outline Confessions	$15.00	
My Life Is A Movie	$15.00	
Represent	$15.00	

SHIPPING/HANDLING: ADD $3.00 per book (Shipped via U.S. Media Mail)

TOTAL: $_____

FORMS OF ACCEPTED PAYMENTS:
Personal checks (additional delays may incur pending bank clearance), institutional checks & money orders are preferred methods of payment. Total Package Publications, LLC does NOT recommend sending cash through the postal system. All mail-in orders take 5-7 business days to be delivered.
Contact Total Package Publications, LLC directly about discounting availability for special bulk orders (ten book minimum).